LOST

K. LUCAS

SHADOW
PRESS

BY ACCIDENT . . . OR DESIGN?

K. LUCAS

EBook ISBN: 978-1-958445-04-4

Paperback ISBN: 978-1-958445-05-1

Hardback ISBN: 978-1-958445-06-8

Cover Design by Pretty In Ink Creations

Editing and Proofreading by My Brother's Editor

In loving memory of my dearest dog, Boo.
2007—2022

I'll always miss petting your soft fur,
playing with your floppy velvet ears,
feeling your gentle lick against my toes,
cuddling with you for hours while your warm breath puffs
against me,
watching you playfully chase the birds across the yard,
and so many other beautiful things.

May you rest in peace on the other side of the rainbow bridge
until we meet again.
I love you, girl.

PART 1

ERIN

CHAPTER ONE

THIS IS PROBABLY *the dumbest idea I've had yet.* My stomach roils as the ship rocks back and forth, more violent with each new wave that crashes against it. I double over, barely making it to the toilet before I cast up the bile from my empty stomach. A moan escapes through my lips as I sit panting on the floor, squeezed inside the tiny bathroom.

"May I have your attention, please?" An announcement comes on through the speakers. "We're going to continue experiencing rough seas as we go around the storm. If you're experiencing sea sickness, you may wish to remain in your cabin, or if you have an interior stateroom, you may wish to go out on deck to get some fresh air. The starboard and port side decks are presently closed, so if you do decide to go outside, please stick to the pool deck. Thank you for your patience as we weather this together."

Another groan slips from my throat at the announcement. *I have the worst possible cabin on this entire ship.* Inside cabin —upper level—back of ship. *Why did I let Marcella talk me into this?*

Just as I have the thought, my phone vibrates on the bed. I

crawl across the floor, afraid that if I stand, I'll hurl again. I reach one arm up over the ledge of the bed to grasp my phone. The screen shows a message.

Come up to the pool.

My eyes drift from the screen to the closed laptop halfway tucked under my pillows. *She can't possibly be writing during this.* I take a few steadying breaths to calm my stomach, then text Marcella back.

I'm too sick.

An instant reply.

It's better up here. Trust me!

I look around my small, windowless cabin. My stomach does another somersault. I'm not sure if I've ever felt this sick in my life. The announcement said to get fresh air. Marcella said it was better up top too, and although it's only a few levels above my current location, I can't help but think anything is better than here. *May as well give it a shot.*

Phone in my pocket, barf bag in hand, I slip carefully into the hallway and make my way to the staircase.

OUTSIDE, the wind is howling. The sound of the waves slamming against our ship is almost too overwhelming to bear.

Water laps over the sides, making me want to turn right back around. If it wasn't for the fresh air instantly soothing my stomach, I would give in to the urge to go back inside.

As it is, I feel somewhat less green—enough to make me cross the deck to where Marcella sits on a lounge chair next to the others. She looks up from her novel as I approach. "Is it that bad?" She grimaces at the bag in my hand.

"Worse. How can you read with all this damned swaying?"

She shrugs. "Born with sea legs, I guess."

I frown, looking at Graham, Tom and Wade, all sitting back in lounge chairs next to her. *All writing away on their laptops.* "I'm so jealous of you guys right now," I say, moving to take an empty seat nearby.

"Didn't spend all that money on a writers' retreat to not write," Graham says without looking up.

Wade and Tom only smile and keep typing.

I scoff but otherwise say nothing. *Some writers' retreat.* I keep my gaze out at the furious ocean, trying not to look at Marcella. She's the only reason I'm sitting here right now, but I don't want to blame her. She didn't know it was going to be like this—she was only trying to help.

"Next time, we know better than to go on a cruise in September," Marcella says cheerily, trying to lighten the mood.

Next time I get a divorce, I'll plan the timing a little better. I bite back the remark. I'm still too angry—too unpleasant to be around. "Have you seen Lauren?" I ask instead.

"She's with Caleb in their room. They both felt sick too, but they have a balcony."

I turn toward her. My eyes widen a little in surprise. "Is it safe?"

She shrugs.

"Maybe you should've thought twice about going on a cruise if you're that afraid," Graham says.

I glare at him, wanting to say something scathing. I want to ask who the hell even invited him. Before I can get anything out, Wade says, "None of us knew about the storm."

My eyes find his still staring at his monitor, and I realize he's not typing. His fingers are poised above the keyboard but are unmoving. I wonder if he's been that way all along and I didn't realize it. *Has he just been pretending to write?*

"That's right," Marcella chimes in. "So quit being such a dick, Graham." She turns to me. "We'll be past the storm soon, and tomorrow we'll be able to get off the ship. It will all be worth it when we get to lie under the shade of a palm tree and type all day long, trust me."

I look up at the gray skies above. "You really think we'll outrun it by tomorrow?"

"That's what the captain said, isn't it?" Graham says.

My face heats. "Do you have a problem with me?"

"No." He pauses. "I have a problem... with *complaining.*"

I stand up on shaky legs. *I don't have to sit here and deal with this.* Graham sounds too much like my husband—*ex*-husband, for me to stand his company any longer. There's nothing that says I have to stay around him. He may be a part of our group, but that's meaningless to me.

"She wasn't complaining!" Marcella cries. "Don't go, Erin."

"No, it's okay. I'm in the mood for a drink anyway."

She glances at the men then back to me. "I'll join you."

"You don't have to."

She hesitates and I don't hold it against her. I don't miss the way her body turns toward Wade, the flush that creeps up her neck when he looks her way, the way she perspires when he talks to her. After all these years, I know when Marcella is interested in a man—and right now she wants Wade.

It doesn't matter that we met him and the others for the first time when we boarded the ship yesterday. I'm not going to judge her, and I'm not going to take the chance to get to know him better away from her. We only have a week on our hands, and I want my friend to make the most of her vacation —not coddle me the whole time.

I walk away before she has the chance to think any more. "I'll catch up with you later," I call.

"Are you sure?" she calls back when I'm several steps away.

I wave a hand in the air, not bothering to look back. It's no big deal. I smile to myself.

CHAPTER TWO

I SIT at one of the several bars aboard the ship, watching the outside water spray the massive window. I take a sip from my glass, relishing the taste and the burn. The bartender was generous—an apology of sorts for the choppy day.

I'm about to get up, move to a spot closer to the window where I can sip my Long Island and listen to an audiobook, when a voice says, "Mind if I join you?"

I turn to see Wade. My stomach drops. *Marcella.* "Sure," I say, torn between wanting solitude but also not wanting to be rude. He orders a beer, and we sit in silence until he says, "Graham is an ass."

I laugh, already loose from the alcohol that my body isn't used to. "I'm over it. It doesn't matter."

Wade nods.

"Did you two know each other already—before this trip?"

"Only through online," he says, referring to the online writing group that we're all a part of.

I nod. "What about the others?"

"Same."

A man of little words.

"You?" he asks.

"Marcella and I have known each other forever. But no, everyone else—this is the first time." I release a breath. "It was scary—the idea of going on a sort of vacation with a bunch of strangers, but exciting too."

He raises an eyebrow. "It's not really supposed to be a vacation."

"Oh, you know what I mean." I wave a hand around. "A writer's retreat on a cruise ship isn't exactly *not* a vacation."

Wade laughs. "Good point." He pauses before asking, "Are you feeling better?"

Heat creeps to my cheeks. I wiggle my glass. "Getting there." And I'm not sure if it's from the heat behind his eyes, or the heat radiating on my face, that makes me say, "So... where's Marcella?"

"Reading," he says, gaze unwavering. "Tom and Graham are still typing away, in case you were wondering."

I open my mouth to say something else, but we're interrupted. "Hey guys!"

Wade and I turn to see Lauren and Caleb holding hands behind us. Lauren is flushed and glowing, Caleb grinning. *Neither looks seasick to me.* "How about that storm? Gnarly, right?" Caleb says.

I give him a tight smile. "Tell that to my stomach."

"I have a friend who works on board," Lauren says. "Do you want me to see if he can get you anything? I'm sure they have Dramamine or something."

"No thanks, this is helping some." I hold up my drink, twirling the little umbrella.

"You guys get much writing done?" Caleb asks.

Wade and I share a look. "A little," he says.

"I can't focus in this," I add. "I'm hoping tomorrow I'll be more productive."

"It's our first full day at sea. Don't be so hard on yourself." Caleb smiles at us, kisses Lauren's hand, and takes a step back, pulling her with him.

"We're going up. Catch you later," Lauren says.

Wade turns to me, waiting like he expects me to want to follow after them.

"You don't have to stay here with me. I'm fine, I promise."

"That's not—that's not why I came down here." He sighs. "I'll catch up with you later."

When he stands up to leave, I bite my lip, guilt flooding me. I wasn't trying to push him away, just—"Wait," I say, stopping him. I smile. "Tell me about your book."

He grins. "Which one?"

I laugh. "The one you're writing."

He nods to the chairs by the window. "Let's get more comfortable."

We move from the bar to the cozy seats overlooking the ocean. Wade tells me all about his thriller about a truck driver who's a serial killer and decides to invite his wife on his conquests. It's the most I've heard him speak. Listening to him talk about his work, the way his eyes light up describing his own imagined characters, the way his whole body thrums with excitement—I feel like I could listen to him for hours.

"What about you?" he asks, realizing how much he's been chatting and how little I've been.

"I've actually been—kind of struggling with that," I admit. I bite my lip. "My—ex-husband didn't—" I struggle for the right words. The ones that won't make me cringe from anger and embarrassment.

"It's been a struggle for me to write," I say. "That's why

I'm here. I'm hoping to clear my head and finally get some words to paper." I shrug. "I'm not sure what they'll be."

Wade's lips thin. He nods in understanding. "I'm glad you're free now." He blushes, quickly adding, "I mean to write. To write whatever comes to you."

WADE and I stay at our spot by the window, talking for hours. Somehow we don't run out of things to say to one another. When my glass is drained, he orders me another and then another, never letting me go thirsty. The time slips by without either of us noticing, until the sea outside is no longer visible and I realize the violent rocking of the ship has ebbed.

"We must be past the storm," I say, relieved.

"The worst of it, at least."

My stomach growls and I notice how dark it is outside the large window now. "How long have we been here?"

"A while I guess."

My stomach grumbles again. "I'm starving." I start to stand, but my world spins on its axis. I fall toward Wade, who catches me easily. A drunken laugh slips through my lips.

He smiles.

"I might've had too much to drink," I say in confidence.

"That might be my fault," he admits.

He's still holding me, hasn't let go yet. I stay close to him, relishing the feel of warm arms around me after being lonely for so long. *Divorce is such a long, ugly process.* His hands keep my body steady, but my mind still spins and spins. I lay my head against his chest. Wade's heartbeat speeds beneath my ear. He seems frozen in place, almost holding his breath.

My stomach rumbles again, making me giggle. I pull away, swaying a little. That's when I see Marcella behind him, watching us with a grim expression. I step back in surprise and sway again. Before I can speak, Wade pulls me back to him and bends to kiss me.

CHAPTER THREE

I WAKE UP SWEATING. Alcohol always makes me run hot. I kick the loose blanket off my legs, trying to remember how I wound up in bed. Naked.

I scramble through my small cabin, getting cleaned up and dressed while trying to remember. My stomach is calm today, not sick at all and it dawns on me we're not swaying. *We must be past the storm.* The only thing wrong now is my head pounding.

There are gaps, but I remember drinking with Wade. I remember the kiss. And Marcella—the cold look in her eyes.

My head thrums with pain from too much alcohol. I glance at my laptop, now sitting on top of my suitcase. *I should write today.* I steel myself with determination. I'm *going* to write today. After I check in with the others.

A daily program slipped under the door tells me that today is a port day. I can't help but smile, both relieved and excited to be off the wild ocean and on the warm, still, sandy beach. Paradise. *I'll be able to write for hours and hours.*

I FIND the others by the buffet, already eating breakfast and sipping coffee. "Good morning," I say, pulling up a chair to their already filled table.

They all look so grim. Wade is the only one to respond. "Morning."

"What's wrong with everyone?" I ask. It's obvious there's something they know that I don't. I peer at Marcella, my face heating. *Oh, god, is this something to do with last night?*

"We veered off course," Graham says. "No disembarking today."

"How is *veering off course* even possible on a cruise?"

He scowls. "When the captain decided to take us around the storm—we overshot the mark."

Overshot—the—mark. "Okay... so what now? It's fine, right? The water is calm. We can all still sit outside and write. No big deal?" I look around at their faces, all frowning. This is a letdown—a big one. But there are more days on our trip, more ports to visit and more time to get done what we came here to do—to write.

"The whole point of this was to experience the island life —the culture—everything that goes with it," Graham says.

"I thought you were writing a horror novel about an evil cat," Tom interrupts.

"That's beside the point."

"There *is* still an island," Lauren says, pointing out the window. "We just can't go on it."

I turn to see the most gorgeous island outside, covered in a lush forest, filled with palm trees. White sandy beaches wrap around to the far side, where cliff sides jut out. It looks completely vacant—void of all human life. "Where are we?" I whisper, in awe of the island's beauty.

"Like I said—we veered off course," Graham says dryly.

"So... we're not disembarking—why does it seem like we're sitting still? Shouldn't we be moving on to correct our course?"

"According to Lauren's—friend," Caleb interjects, giving her a look. "We're going to be *parked* here all day. The captain is giving everyone's stomachs some time to settle before we're back at it again. The storm is still brewing where we're *supposed* to be, so this will give it some time to pass too."

"How considerate of him," Graham says, his words laced with sarcasm.

I look back at Marcella, who still hasn't said a word. *She can't really be that angry, can she?* I sigh. It's always been this way with her. If a man she's interested in *isn't* interested in her—it's because of me. It doesn't matter if it's *actually* because of me, or not.

"Right. Well, during this interlude, while I'm not throwing up all over myself—"

"Or getting drunk," Marcella says.

I ignore her. "I'm going to make the most of it. I'll be on Deck D writing my ass off. Unless there are people there—then you can find me on another deck." I stand, all appetite gone.

"Wait," Caleb says.

I stop and turn toward him.

"That's not all Lauren's friend had to say." He nods toward my seat, inviting me to stay and hear him out. I indulge him.

"Andrew says—" Lauren starts, lowering her voice and looking at each of us. "That even though we're not *supposed* to disembark, he can get us on a *tender*." She waits expectantly for one of us to speak.

"And what is that—exactly?" I ask, new to all the cruise ship terminology.

"A lifeboat," Wade says.

"A—"

We all look at each other. *They want to sneak off the ship.* I can't tell if the others think it's a crazy idea or brilliant. I don't even know what *I* think about it. My heart races. It could be dangerous—the island looks uninhabited. It could also be the most peaceful place I'll ever visit on this planet. *I could write a book about this experience alone, probably.* I can almost see the idea in the others' eyes.

"Are you sure the ship is going to stay all day?" I ask Lauren.

She nods.

"You can't be seriously considering this," Graham says. "The captain will know. We'll be caught."

"Andrew says he has a few others willing to help. They'll distract the captain, make sure no one else knows about it—if —we can pay." Her cheeks redden at the admission, realizing how it sounds.

Graham throws his arms up and scoffs.

"We can pay them half up front and half when we're safely back," Caleb says.

"How much do they want?" I ask, thinking about the divorce that cost me everything, about the airplane ticket and stateroom that I couldn't afford because my ex-husband had a better attorney.

"Forget the money for a second. Think about the safety. What if something happens? We're *writers*. None of us knows anything about survival—" Graham starts, but Marcella cuts him off.

"Survival?" she barks. "What's there to *survive*, Graham? It's a *beach*!" She looks at each of us. "I'm in. I don't care about the added cost. This is a once-in-a-lifetime opportunity. I'm in. We'll leave and be back before bedtime."

"What about the other ports? We still have plenty of opportunities to disembark," I say.

"Not like this, and you know it."

I look at Wade, deciding I'll go whichever way he leans. If he thinks it's a stupid idea, then I'll stay. If he wants to go, then I will too. I'm not sure why, but he seems to be one of the most level-headed here. There's something about him that I trust. It's not because of last night—it's more like last night might've happened because of it.

He seems to be trying to read me, just like I am him. After a minute, he says, "If we're really going to do this, we better get going."

CHAPTER FOUR

THE PLAN IS HATCHED SO QUICKLY, so thoroughly, that I wonder how many times this friend of Lauren's has snuck passengers off the ship. He and the others helping have to be making a small fortune off passengers willing to disembark on their own—like us.

There's not much in way of preparation—nothing for us to pack other than our computers and sunblock. Lauren and Marcella each have clear, waterproof backpacks they thought to bring. I make a stop by the buffet with my canvas bag to stock up on water bottles. The humidity has me drinking water like a fish, and I don't want a little thirst to get in the way of a full day's writing.

Everything comes together within an hour, and now I hang on for dear life as the lifeboat jumps wave after wave in the angry water. There's no storm, but it doesn't matter. The size of the small boat is so different from the colossal cruise ship, we can't help but feel every bounce and jolt that comes our way. Water that seemed calm and still moments ago, is now giving us a different story.

"Few more minutes," Lauren's friend calls to us, noting how we all look a little queasy from the jostling.

If I speak, I know I'll lose the little control of my stomach that I have left, so I stay silent. We all do for a while. Wind whips past us, and slowly, the beautiful island grows larger as our ship shrinks in the distance. My heart hammers faster the longer we're gone. *We're actually doing this!*

Despite how my stomach feels, I grin. I can't help it. I feel freer than I ever have in my entire existence. This is *exactly* the kind of thing I would've *never* been able to do with Matt. If I had even *suggested* it, even looked like I wanted to go along with the plan—he would've shot me down in an instant.

"You look happy," Wade calls from where he's seated across from me.

"I am."

"You're not the only one!" Caleb screams with a hoot and howl. We all laugh at his excitement.

"How are we supposed to get on land?" Graham calls to Andrew.

"There's a small dock around the side of the island."

The others and I all look at each other in confusion.

Andrew says, "This island was abandoned by the cruise line years ago. You might see some tiki umbrellas and beach chairs. There's even a bathroom somewhere, but I'm not sure what state it's in, so you might want to avoid it."

"Is there a bar?" Caleb grins.

Andrew laughs. "No bar, unfortunately. No food either, so I hope you all brought snacks."

"What kind of cruise-line-owned island doesn't have a bar?" Tom says.

"The kind that's too small, too hard to get to, too unprofitable to maintain," Andrew says. "I don't know all the details, sorry, man. All I know is this place used to be one of the stops during peak season, years and years ago—an exclusive VIP thing for rich guys. That's how I know about the dock. It closed down for storm season, and eventually, they just washed their hands of it." He makes a hand-washing gesture to emphasize his point.

We accept Andrew's words at face value even though none of us have ever heard of something like that. He's the employee, he'd know more about it than us, although the writer in me insists I should look more into it when I get back to the ship and get some internet.

When we're almost to the dock, Andrew says, "Remember, we won't be back to get you until nightfall. Stay out of view of the ship, so no one sees you—unless you want your little excursion cut short."

"And if we have a problem?" Graham asks.

"I'll leave you with a flare gun and a pack of flares, but please—do not use the damn thing unless someone is *dying*. All our jobs are on the line here, not to mention I'm not sure what kind of charges you all will face." He gives us all a pointed look.

"Yeah, we get it," Graham says.

We pull up to the dock.

"Let's get to it then, shall we?" Tom says, the first to leave.

We pile out after him, computers and bags in hand.

"Lauren's friend said we should stay out of sight of the ship," Marcella says once we're all off the dock.

Graham stops. He looks across the sea to our ship. Only the back is visible from where we are. "Do you think anyone will even be able to see us if they looked?"

"Is it worth the risk?" She glares at him.

WE MAKE our way across the beach, to where the island starts to curve around at a sharper angle. The ship isn't completely out of view, but far enough now to where we know we won't be seen unless someone is specifically looking for us.

I gasp when I see the tiki umbrellas lined up on the sand. "Andrew was right."

"Of course he was. Did you think he was lying?" Lauren says.

"No, I just—"

"You think these chairs will hold us up?" Caleb says. He puts his weight on one of the beach chairs, gradually pushing down until it's fully supporting him. He gives a little bounce and laughs. "I'll be damned."

We all settle ourselves into our ideal spots. Caleb, Lauren, and Marcella stay in the open, as close to the water as they can get without the tide getting them. Lauren grins at me as she puts tanning oil on, and I can't help but grin back.

Graham and Tom somehow look the most comfortable of all of us. They've pulled beach chairs back a ways, just at the outskirts of the forest. On a small hill, they're overlooking the rest of us like kings.

Wade hesitates. "Do you—want to sit together?"

I smile at his shyness. "Yes. How about over there?" I lead him to a spot near a single palm tree that's reaching sideways into the sky. We're still within sight of the others but far enough away that we don't have to hear them.

"This is perfect," he says, making himself comfortable. I

do the same, sitting across from him so that our bare toes could touch if one of us reached. I finally open my laptop and start to write.

WE SPEND the rest of the day working. A few hours pass before we start to toss ideas back and forth with each other and the others in the group. We're all writing different genres, but it doesn't matter—the input from other writers is invaluable. I've been looking for this comradery since I can remember. I feel complete, like everything that brought me to this point has been worth it.

None of us has a signal to get internet, so if there's something we need to research, we ask, and if no one knows, we make a note to look it up later. Hours fly by us in a blur. It amazes me how productive we can be when the only sounds around us are the birds and the waves.

"My battery is getting low," Wade says later. The sun is setting, almost down completely.

"Mine is too." The built-in batteries, along with the portable chargers we brought, are all drained.

"Ready to stop for the day?"

I finish the paragraph that I'm working on, then save my work and close my computer. We each pack up and get ready to move toward the others, but Wade stops me. He beams. "It was great working with you."

I smile back. "It was perfect." I start to turn, but he grabs my arm.

"About last night—"

By now, I remember everything, and it's hard to look him

in the eyes when he mentions it. Wade brought me back to my room after the kiss, I tried to seduce him, and he politely declined. He made sure I was safe and left. That was that. I blacked out after flopping onto the bed, disappointed and too drunk to be embarrassed.

Now that I've had a chance to sober up and the memory had a chance to surface, I'm mortified. I can't stand the way I treated a complete stranger who's supposed to be a colleague —who I'm now supposed to spend a week with. He came onto me with the kiss, but I should've stopped it at that instead of wanting to jump into bed.

"You don't have to say anything," I say, turning scarlet. "I'm sorry. I drank too much—I should've been more responsible. I apologize."

He runs a hand through his hair and shakes his head. "No. You don't—"

A scream fills the air. Our heads whip toward the others.

"What the hell! What the hell!" Marcella is wailing in the water up to her thighs, staring out at the ocean.

We drop everything and run for her.

"What's wrong?" Tom asks, getting to her first.

She turns back, wide eyed and crying, looking like a frightened wild animal. "The ship—it's *gone*!"

CHAPTER FIVE

WE ALL STARE out at the spot our cruise ship should be. The spot it *was* just a few hours earlier. *How could we not have noticed it leaving?*

"Let's not panic," Tom says. "We need to walk back down the beach first." He turns to Graham. "Do you still have the flare gun?"

"Maybe this is part of the plan?" Lauren says before Graham can answer, starting to look just as panicked as Marcella. "Andrew said he'd come back at night—maybe he will still."

I choke on her words. *Maybe. Maybe he'll come back for us.* My world is starting to spin. I blink, trying to clear the dizzy haze from my eyes. Black spots are at the corners of my vision, creeping in faster and faster until I find myself falling to the sand.

"Shit," Graham growls. He's the closest to me and reaches out to catch me before I hit my head. He holds me for a moment, steadying me, making sure I'm not going to fall again. It's the worry I see on his face that's more frightening than anything else. If he's worried—*we all should be.*

TOGETHER, we trek back down the beach to the spot we arrived. When we still don't see the ship, I break out in a cold sweat. We keep going, hoping that maybe the ship isn't gone completely—it could've just moved, floated away maybe. *Anything but this.*

We walk until the sun is completely down, the only light the looming rays on the water. "It's gone," Marcella says, dropping to her knees. "We're—*stranded.*"

"Don't say that," Caleb barks at her. "Andrew will come through. We just have to stay calm."

I look at Lauren, who's biting her lip. "How—" I don't want to call her out. I know this isn't her fault. But I can't help but ask. "How do you know Andrew?"

All eyes turn to her. We wait on pins and needles for her to say something—anything to reassure us that we didn't just put our lives in the hands of a con man. "It's not what you think," she says. "I met him at a party—we hooked up." Her eyes flash to Caleb before continuing. "That was months ago, way before Caleb. And we've just been friends since."

We let out a collective sigh of relief. She didn't just meet him. She knows him. Most importantly, we can probably trust him. *Then what's with the look on her face saying she's not so sure?*

"There's something you're not telling us," Tom says, seeing the look too.

Lauren shakes her head. "No. I swear that's it."

"Then why do you still look so worried?" Graham asks.

"It's just—the ship wasn't supposed to move." Tears fall

from her eyes now as she stares at us. "It wasn't supposed to leave."

The words hit us like a blow to the gut, knocking the air from each of our lungs. We really are stranded. I look at Wade, who's looking out to sea. Marcella starts yelling at Lauren and lunges for her hair while the others hold her back. It's not her or Caleb's fault, but how can we not blame them a little?

Nausea overcomes me. I run a few feet away before doubling over, spilling my guts into the sand. *This isn't happening. This isn't happening!*

Wade speaks loud and clear so we can all hear him over our panic. "We need to try making a fire. It's going to get cold tonight, and if that storm we went around heads our way, we're going to wish we had a shelter."

"He's right," Graham says. "We have to stay smart." He looks at Wade with approval. "I'll help gather some wood."

I feel like I'm stumbling through a nightmare, trying to wake up, but instead, the monster is about to get me. *Matt, where are you when I need you?* I blink, trying to focus. Wade and Graham are right. Their words are rational—they make sense. And yet, I feel like if we do this—if we *set up camp*, we're giving in. We're going to accept that we are alone on this island—trapped with no escape.

"How can we just accept this?" I cry, feeling like we're all on the edge of a cliff, the ground is shaking, and no one wants to hang on. "There has to be something else we can do!" I turn to Graham, frantic. "Shoot the flare."

He starts to shake his head, but I don't give him the chance. I go to him, pulling at the bag slung over his shoulder. "Where is it?" I demand, clawing my way to the zipper.

"Hold on a minute—"

"No! Shoot it now! Before it's too late!" Hands are on me,

pulling me back, but it takes all of them to combat my thrashing arms. "Just shoot it!" I cry as they pull me away.

Marcella speaks up behind me. "She's right! Shoot the damn thing. What can it hurt?"

I stop struggling, and they let me go. I back away from everyone, taking deep breaths to give someone—anyone a chance to speak. Everyone's eyes search each other's as if in a silent consultation. I bite my lip while I wait, drawing blood from clenching down too hard.

"Should we—" Caleb starts.

It's Wade who says, "No."

My eyes dart to him, unable to believe he would be against this.

"The ship is gone. We know it's gone, or we would see it—even on the horizon. If we shoot it, it's wasted."

Marcella starts to protest, but he continues. "We need to save it for when they come looking."

There's a grim expression on his face. He doesn't like the words any more than anyone else.

"Listen, if we're not going to use the flare to try to get rescued, maybe we can still put it to good use. We can use it to start a fire," Tom says.

My heart lurches. *Yes!* Finally someone is thinking around here! "That's a perfect idea!"

Graham shakes his head again. "The whole point is to save the flares for when we really need them. When there's a chance of rescue, we shoot them. If we waste them all, we're going to be shit out of luck later on."

"How can you say it's *wasting*?" I reel myself back, on the verge of lashing out at him. I cannot comprehend what's happening right now. He and Wade aren't seeing reason and there's no way for me to make them. They're trying to convince everyone that their way is best when it's far from it.

"It would only take one to start a fire. *One.*" I search every-one's faces, trying to meet their eyes. Marcella knows what I mean. I can see it on her face that she agrees. Caleb is on the fence but close to agreeing too.

"Andrew entrusted me with the gun. He said to only use it if someone was dying. Until we have that kind of situation on our hands, I'm saving the flares." He walks away from the group, end of discussion.

I'm stunned, angry, disappointed. The others shrug it off like it doesn't matter. Wade looks relieved to not have to debate about it anymore. I can't look at him, can't look at any of them. That they're willing to continue going without a fire, for fear of going against what *Andrew* said—it's unbelievable. Until I can get the gun from Graham, though, there's not much I can do about it except hope they're able to get a fire started another way.

CHAPTER SIX

ONCE THE SUN is completely down, the dark envelops us more than any of us imagined. It's more black, more pure, than we've ever experienced, and frankly, more terrifying. We use what's left of the batteries on our phones to shine enough light to see. Wade and Graham struggle to build a fire, while Caleb and the rest of us use the tiki umbrellas and palm leaves to make a half-ass shelter that will keep a little of the wind out without falling on top of us.

"Don't any of you smoke?" Graham calls to us, wiping the sweat from his brow. They got to work trying to start the fire almost as soon as we realized no one was coming for us. It's been hours now, and not even a spark.

When he asks the question, an image of my ex-husband flashes before my eyes. *Matt grins at me, holding a cigar between his teeth.* I shake my head, banishing the picture of him from my thoughts. "I don't. Do you guys?" I ask, already knowing that Marcella vapes and doesn't have a lighter. *The flare gun would sure make an easy job of it.*

"He's already asked this three times," Lauren says, irritated.

I nod. I deserve to be snapped at. While the others got immediately to work, I stayed away, wallowing in my own self-pity instead of doing something about it, until Tom finally came to get me and see if I was okay. So I say nothing now to Lauren and continue to help in any way I can, any way they need me.

"I need more palm leaves on this side," Marcella says.

"We just used the last one," Lauren answers with a huff.

"I'll go get more," I say, heading for the edge of the forest. I take a few steps when my phone dings at me. I hold my breath, flooded with adrenaline. *I might have a signal. We can call for help!*

But it's just an alert—low battery. I look up at the others, who are staring at me wide eyed, waiting. They see the disappointment on my face and get back to work while I step beyond the trees.

IT'S hard to do things one-handed, especially dragging stacks of giant palm leaves out of a forest and across the sand, while feeling like every wild animal is watching me—waiting for an opportunity to attack. The light on my phone starts to dim as it makes its last attempts to reserve battery life. As my glowing ring of light shrinks, fear creeps up my spine at the idea of being alone in the dark.

A branch breaks in the distance, and I freeze. I wait, holding my fading light up to see around me. Bugs buzz around the light, swarming toward the beacon. *Is it Graham getting more firewood?*

Another crack in the forest. A rustle—closer this time. I drop my stack of leaves and run.

I'm not slow—I run every morning, and I know how to haul ass. But this—whatever it is—has no problem keeping pace with me. I blow through the edge of the forest onto the sand, gasping for air.

"What's wrong?" Tom asks, hurrying to me.

"Did you get the leaves?" Lauren says, not noticing or not caring that something's wrong.

I take a few more steps away from the trees, looking over my shoulder to be sure. "There was something in there," I gasp, still trying to catch my breath.

"What was it?" Caleb asks.

"I don't know. It was—I think it was chasing me." I look at them to gauge their reaction, then past them. "Where's Marcella?"

"She went to help you," Lauren says.

I look back at the edge of the trees with wide eyes. *Was that Marcella I heard?* "She—" *But why was she chasing me?*

As if reading my mind, Tom says, "That was probably just her that you heard. It's okay." He puts a hand on my shoulder. I know he's trying to comfort me, but it rubs me the wrong way, like he's being condescending to me.

I take a step away and say to Caleb, "I'm sorry. I got spooked and dropped what I had."

He sighs and runs a hand through his blond hair. "It's okay. We should've never let you go in alone."

"You all were working on the shelter. It was the least I could do."

"It doesn't matter. It's dark now, and who knows what the hell is on this island. No one goes in alone, especially at night, from now on. Agreed?" He looks between me, Lauren, and Tom, and we nod our heads.

I like this side of Caleb—not the carefree, fun-loving guy who was on the ship, but a new, serious, take-charge Caleb. He's down to business now that it matters, and I admire his ability to take our situation seriously.

The writer side of me can't help but wonder what genre Caleb writes. I thought maybe something with comedy, but now I'm not so sure. I should know better than to assume an author's genre based on their personality. There's another side to him that's not so obvious at first. I wonder what's not so obvious about everyone else.

AFTER A FEW MINUTES, when Marcella still hasn't come back, we make our way to Graham, a couple hundred yards from the tree line. He hadn't looked up or even flinched when I came bolting out of the forest, and he's still rubbing his sticks together, trying to get a fire started.

"Where's Wade?" I ask in between his curses.

"He went to grab more tinder."

"... Where?"

"Where do you think?" he snaps.

"Hey man, that's—" Tom starts.

Graham says, "He went into the forest."

I meet Caleb's eyes, then look back at Graham. "How long ago?"

"I don't know. Twenty minutes? Now if you don't mind, I'm trying to get us some goddamn heat."

I feel like my face is on fire. I walk away slowly, unable to meet anyone's gaze. As I leave, I hear Lauren say, "Good for her! She's been eyeing him from the minute we stepped onto the ship!"

I'm so stupid. I never should've kissed him. I never should've interfered. Not when I knew she had her eye on him. *No wonder he turned me down.*

I tell myself it doesn't matter. It's nothing. I'm getting over a *divorce,* for crying out loud. I am *not* upset over this. Just embarrassed. That's all.

CHAPTER SEVEN

Wade and Marcella come back separately, him first, followed by her a few minutes later. He's a picture of innocence, carrying the tinder that he's promised, not even glancing my way. She's grinning from ear to ear.

I feel sick to my stomach the rest of the night. I remind myself I haven't eaten dinner—of course I would feel sick from skipping a meal. It has nothing to do with the look on Marcella's face, and definitely not with the way she moved from helping us with the shelter, to helping Graham and Wade with the fire.

They're not able to get one started, despite all the effort put into it. We're forced to huddle together through the night —all seven of us. The men insist one of us women get between each of them to *prevent weirdness*, but I'm not sure if it makes things less weird or more so.

Somehow, I wind up between Graham and Wade— Marcella on Wade's other side, *of course*. I want to say something—say I'd rather take Caleb's or Tom's body heat, but I don't want to be childish and don't want to make things more awkward than they already are.

It doesn't matter who the hell I sleep next to, I scold myself. *We are stranded on a fucking island. Nothing else matters.*

I OPEN my eyes this morning, almost sweating from the heat radiating off the two men next to me. Wade is wrapped around my back, his arm holding my shoulder, and my head is against Graham's chest, his arm lying across my thigh.

They're pressed in so close, I have to bite my lip to keep from moving. If I move backward, away from Graham—Wade might not be able to breathe. If I move forward, toward Graham and away from Wade—I don't want to think about it.

I can't help but smile to myself. *Never thought I'd be in a position like this.* A picture of Matt pops into my head. I clench my eyes shut, trying to embrace the heat against the cold morning air, trying not to think of them as men, but as warm bodies—warmth—survival.

Graham's fingers twitch against me, and despite his attitude, despite him being a complete asshole, I want to lean toward him. *Just a little.* It doesn't matter who he is—what he is. I want to *feel.* Feel anything but this overwhelming sense of regret and failure.

I clench my eyes tighter, but only last two minutes before I rise, trying not to wake the others. I have to clear my head, my thoughts, everything that doesn't matter. *How are we going to get off this island?*

"DID YOU FIND ANYTHING HELPFUL?" Graham asks me, bent over his sticks, trying once again to start the fire. He's the only one awake when I get back from jogging down the beach.

I blush when I see him, the memory of my traitorous thoughts from earlier coming back. I look away, hoping he thinks my red face is just from exercise, but I swear he's smiling to himself. *Don't acknowledge it. He's goading you.*

"No," I say. "Nothing but shoreline. Still no ship."

"No sign of Lauren's friend?"

"No. None that I saw."

"I knew we were stupid to trust him."

Anger rises in me. He's right, but it doesn't matter. There's something about his attitude—something that just *bugs* me. I can't help but turn back toward him. "Why did you?"

He shrugs. "She said she knew him from before."

"But she didn't say that until we were already here."

His gaze finally meets mine. "I was just going along for the ride. No sense meeting a bunch of strangers for a writing retreat and not sticking with them when they're going to write." His eyebrows arch as if to challenge me.

I'm not sure if I believe him. Graham seems like the kind of person to never just *go along* with anything. But he also has no reason to lie. *As far as I know.*

Movement comes behind us. The others are awake. "Did anyone pack any water?" Marcella croaks. Her raspy voice makes me realize how thirsty I am too.

"We should take inventory of what we all have," Caleb says.

It's a good idea, and all of us move to open our bags and get whatever meager supplies we brought with us. Even Graham stops trying to build the fire to join us.

"This can't be everything," Marcella says when we've all emptied everything we have.

"We didn't exactly have groceries for a picnic," I say. "We were on a *cruise.*"

She glares at me. We still haven't spoken after she saw Wade kiss me on the ship. There's a rift between us, and I'm trying to set it aside for the greater good here, but she can't seem to look past it. "I know *exactly* where we were," she says.

We all stare at the small pile before us—a bottle of water for each of us, a bag of chips, and a small bottle of rum—not one of those mini bottles like they give on airplanes, but no bigger than a water bottle. "What are we going to eat?" Lauren cries, falling to her knees.

My stomach growls. I try to clear my throat, trying to ignore the dryness. I'm more worried about fresh water at this point. We have a bottle each between us—that's not even enough for a day. And when we exert ourselves, we need more.

"We need to get the fire going," Graham says, heading back to his sticks.

"Better get on that since we can't use the flare gun to start one," I say, lacing every word with venom. To the others, I add, "We need water."

"We have—" Marcella starts.

"One bottle each isn't enough for long," Caleb cuts her off. "And look at them—none are full."

I give him a look of thanks. He nods. "I'll go with you. We need to find fresh water."

Wade scowls. "It could be dangerous."

"It's worth the risk," I say. "We're going to die if we don't get water."

We all look at each other, waiting for someone to have a reasonable objection, waiting for some other idea or suggestion. No one says a word, though. We're all on the same page. We need a fire, and we need water.

CHAPTER EIGHT

HOW BIG IS this damned island? We've been walking through this forest for hours and still haven't run into any sign of fresh water. Although we probably haven't gotten as far as we think because of how thick the foliage is.

I never thought I'd find myself in a forest on a deserted island, but here I am. *There's a first time for everything, right?* At least it's daytime.

Beams of sunlight shine between the trees, lighting our way. I stay close to Caleb, listening for any sign of the sounds I heard last night. Just in case—in case it wasn't Wade and Marcella that I heard after all. *Something was chasing me.*

"Keep your eye out for something to eat," Caleb says, leading me uphill.

I don't answer. I'm too thirsty for that. We've been trying to not talk to each other, and there's an unspoken understanding between us to only do so when absolutely necessary. I'm not sure why he felt the need to remind me about food since he knows we're both starving, and I try not to be irritated with him for the comment.

We continue our uphill trek until something catches my

eye. "Wait," I call. There's movement again. This time Caleb sees it too. "There," I whisper.

A flock of birds is covering the ground, blending in with the forest floor. They're huddled close together, almost indistinguishable, quietly cooing. It's an amazing sight to see—so many little birds, all gathered in one spot so low.

But more importantly—I see what they're eating. "Bananas!" I breathe. I've never been so happy to see bananas in my life. My dry mouth waters at the sight, and then I realize the birds are right there. *Maybe we could—* "Do you think we can catch some of them?"

I thought Caleb would be just as happy as I am, but he wears a grim expression.

"What's wrong?"

"Even if we could catch some of them, they're going to be all bone. Not worth the effort or calories we'll spend trying. And how are we going to get the bananas down?"

I tilt my head back, following his gaze up the tree. The fruit has to be at least twenty feet high—maybe higher. He might be right about the birds, but we can't pass the fruit. "We can ask the others for help."

He doesn't like it. "It took us this long to get here... we're really going to go back to them empty-handed?"

"What else are we supposed to do? And we won't be empty-handed. We still need to find water."

We stare at the birds and banana trees a few more minutes, trying to think of a way—*any* way to get the fruit. We're too tired already, and without knowing how much farther the water is, we agree to come back for the fruit later.

ANOTHER THIRTY MINUTES of walking and we're almost dead on our feet. "Are we turned around?" I ask. "Do we even know which direction we're headed? Or are we walking in blind circles?"

It's so hard not to take my frustration out on Caleb. He's the one leading the way, after all. Even though I tell myself *he's just as thirsty and tired as I am*, it doesn't make me feel any better.

He glares at me, unspeaking. Then his eyes go wide. "Listen!" he hisses.

I hold my breath, straining to hear whatever he's heard. My heart is hammering in my ears, and I will it to calm down so I can focus. A second ticks by, and then another. And then —I hear it. The sound of water.

It's so faint, I'm barely able to catch it, but it's there, in the distance. "A river?" I whisper.

Caleb shakes his head. "No. Probably something smaller like a stream. We'll have to be quiet to find it."

"Do you think it'll be clean enough to drink?"

"If it's flowing, it should be."

"What about you know—" I grimace. "*Animal poop.*"

Caleb rolls his eyes at me. "We'll have to look, but it should be fine. Flowing water is the most important thing."

I have no idea how he can tell, but I don't really care either. All I can think is *fresh water*, because I was starting to doubt that we would find any at all. I follow him in silence the rest of the way, hoping and praying that our ears aren't deceiving us.

CHAPTER NINE

By the time Caleb and I get back to camp, the sun is almost down. I expected to smell the smoke of a campfire, but I don't. Because there *is no fire*. Still, I had also hoped that someone might've found something to eat, and from the looks of it— they haven't.

Caleb and I give each other a look as we come back to the camp, now with a completed shelter and the rest of our group lying in the sand. *No one is doing anything*. A burning rage runs through me, igniting my blood. One look at Caleb tells me he feels the same.

We're too tired, too hungry to be nice. For a split second, I want to chug all the water we managed to carry, right in front of the others. They can watch me quench my thirst and then hike for hours to go get their own. Before I can do anything stupid, I set the water down.

"We're back," Caleb calls, not trying to hide his irritation.

"Water?" Lauren croaks, unmoving.

"Any luck with that fire?" he asks, ignoring her question.

"Any luck finding food?" I ask no one in particular.

No one answers.

Tom is the first to get up, and when I see him, it hits me how thirsty they all must really be. Caleb and I drank our fill after hiking all day, but they haven't been able to after building the shelter and trying to do everything else. The bottle apiece we had was gone too soon.

"Thank you," Tom says from between chapped lips.

I soften. "We found a banana tree. We just have to find a way to get them down. There were little birds too, tons of them, but Caleb thinks maybe they'd be a wasted effort."

Tom takes his fill of the water, then says, "He might be right about the birds. Where are the bananas? I'll go now."

I shake my head. It's getting dark, Caleb and I are both too tired to show him the way, but my stomach growls, making me think twice. *We're going to starve to death in no time if we don't get some food.* "How will you get them down?" I ask instead.

"I'm going to climb."

"But—what if you fall?"

"I won't. I know what I'm doing." He smiles. "Besides, I'm too hungry to be scared and bananas sound delicious."

"They were green," I say, trying to come up with anything to dissuade him. The idea of him climbing thirty feet or more up a tree is terrifying to me, and in the dark—and I'm not even the one going to be doing it.

Tom chuckles now. "Of course they are." He puts a hand on my shoulder. "You don't have to worry. I might be a writer, but I know what I'm doing. I can climb up there and back down before you know it. I've done it a hundred times."

"In the dark?"

"You bet."

I look to Caleb, hoping for a voice of reason, but he only nods. The others, who are now done drinking their fill have heard our conversation. "I can go with," Marcella offers.

"What if we wait another day? Lauren's friend might come for us tonight and then this would be all for—"

"He's not coming back," Marcella cuts in. "Stop being so blind. Can't you see our situation? We need food before we're all too weak to do anything."

I bite the inside of my lip. *Who am I to stop him if he really wants to do this?*

Marcella turns to Tom. "Are we going or what?"

He nods. "I'm ready." He turns to Caleb and me. "Which way are we heading?"

"If you're going, the stream we found isn't far from there," Caleb says. "You should try to bring back more water too, if you can."

"How far?" Marcella asks.

"It took us hours to find the bananas," I say. "The stream wasn't much farther."

They look at each other, finally getting the point that I was trying to make. *Hours in the dark. Climbing a tree—in the dark.* "Let's go," Tom says. They gather a few bottles we've already emptied and head back into the forest.

LATER, I lie on the sand, close to the water, watching the tide roll in. Wade comes to sit next to me. "Thanks for finding water for the group. You probably saved our lives."

"Yep." I stand and move farther down the beach, having no desire to be alone with him. Once I'm settled again, I see him in my peripheral vision, watching me. He's weighing coming to try again with dropping it. *I really hope he drops it.*

I'm exhausted and not in the mood for this. There's nothing to say.

A minute passes. Wade stands, waits, then heads in my direction. I almost groan as he approaches, bracing myself to stand again the minute he sits down.

"We're really alone," he says, standing next to me, understanding I'll move again.

I'm not sure what to say—what he wants me to say, so I don't speak at all.

"Erin, are you okay?"

"Fine."

"You don't seem fine." He places a hand on my shoulder, and I shrug it off. I stand, ready to walk away and avoid this entire situation. "Wait," he says.

I spin on him out of patience. "You said it yourself, Wade. We're alone. We might die here because we all made the stupid decision to trust another human being. He's not coming back for us. Nothing else matters now besides surviving."

He starts to reach for me, but I put up a hand to stop him. "Don't touch me," I say.

Wade reels back, hurt by my words and my tone, but I don't care. I need to hurt him, to cut him so I can release some of my own anger. "Why don't you meet Marcella again to relieve some of the pressure?" It's a low blow, uncalled for, childish—but the words spill out of me before I can stop them. I take off down the beach, more alone now than ever.

CHAPTER TEN

I WAKE in the night with a full bladder, finding that I'm somehow sleeping between Wade and Graham *again*. This time, I'm facing the opposite way—toward Wade now instead of Graham. His breath comes in slow puffs, so close I can feel it against my cheek.

Our conversation comes back to me—my scathing words to him. *It's for the best.*

Graham is pressed up against my back so close, it's as if we're one body. I close my eyes and allow myself a brief moment to relax against him. I feel his warmth, his surprisingly solid chest, his body heat against me.

As Graham's chest rises and falls in a steady pattern against my back, I nestle closer at the comfort. *He's such a jerk, but oh, how comfy.* There's no connection with him, only another body, nothing to make things complicated. I allow myself to imagine that I'm leaning against Matt, warm in bed, *at home,* instead of here. *Nothing's changed. We haven't grown apart. He hasn't forgotten I exist.*

It's been so long—too long since I've been held. I wouldn't consider this being held, really, but it's close enough. Especially with Graham, who I don't particularly even like.

I try not to think about Matt for long, but it's nearly impossible. He could be in the same room as me and not even know I was there, would be too concerned with work. *I could strip naked in front of him, and he wouldn't—no.*

I stop my train of thought before my blood starts to boil. It's over now. It doesn't matter anymore. Longing for my old life will do no one any good.

As I inch forward away from Graham, his arm tightens, stopping me. My breath catches at the surprise, my heartbeat increases.

"You don't have to leave," he breathes in my ear. Goose-flesh rises on my arms. I've never heard this tone from him—he's been a jerk for days; *I'm surprised he's even interested... Okay, maybe not that surprised.*

I pause for a moment, considering what he's offering. I could be reading him wrong. Maybe he's referring to body heat—but his fingers start to move up my body, slowly, and I know it's not body heat he wants.

My eyes pop open. *Wade is right here.* "I can't," I whisper. I try to rise again, but he holds me back again.

"We can move," he says, reading my mind.

It's tempting. So tempting. Even though I don't like him—it doesn't matter. Who needs to like someone in order to *feel?* Feel something other than fear, isolation, loneliness. I'm so... lost. *Maybe it will be better because we don't like each other.*

Graham waits patiently for me to say something, and I'm sure he can feel my racing pulse where his fingers brush against my neck. I'm about to say *okay,* but as I open my mouth to speak the word, Wade opens his eyes.

There's nothing between us. I don't owe him a damn thing, especially after his little meeting with Marcella in the forest. He literally has zero claim on me, or I on him, and I made it crystal clear yesterday, but for some stupid reason, I *do* care what he thinks. There's no doubt now that he's heard Graham's whispers.

Wade stares at me, waiting just like Graham for me to speak. I'm tempted to say *okay* still. *Why shouldn't I?* Hell, maybe I should just ask Wade to join us and really spice things up. No, I can't do that. The difference is that he seems more inclined to care, and after Matt, I can't do that right now.

My decision finally made, I roll over to face Graham, my back now to Wade. I bring a hand up to Graham's face and stroke the stubble on his cheek. I brush his long hair away from his ear and whisper so quietly I'm not sure I even hear myself speak.

"Rain check." Then I get up before he can stop me again.

AFTER LEAVING the shelter to relieve my aching bladder, I sit on the beach and stare at the still-empty firepit. My stomach growls as I watch a crab scuttle across the sand. We need to set some traps. We need to do something else to get more food or we're going to starve. Bananas aren't enough.

I play with the idea of writing. There's still a little battery life on my laptop—I could pop it open for some late-night word count. It might help me clear my thoughts, but I don't think I could focus if I tried.

There's a sliver of an idea, a *grain* of something that's gnawing. It's what I've been working on so far, but I think about the little life my battery has and don't dare waste it.

Instead, I decide to brainstorm ideas about characters and different ways the plot might take me. If I can get the baseline down, even a rough outline in my mind, I can make the most of what I have left of the computer. Who knows how long I'll have to go without charging it.

It's been so long since I've written—since before Matt and I got married. I'm rusty, but rusty is okay. None of that matters, anyway. What matters is getting the story down. I just have to figure out where I'm going with it.

I stay awake for hours, lying on the sand, thinking. Every now and then, I think I hear noises coming from the trees behind me. Something rustles, and I sit up to stare blindly into the dark. When I do, everything goes quiet, and I know I'm being watched.

There's some kind of animal on this island, and I'm afraid to find out what it is and what it wants. We could be in its territory, unwanted invaders. Will it attack us or allow us a temporary stay? Out here alone, I feel vulnerable—like a target with a beacon.

I've had enough brainstorming for one night. I go back to the shelter, where the others are long passed out, and move to the other side to lie next to Tom.

CHAPTER ELEVEN

A MORNING JOG is exactly what I needed. My bare feet hit the soft white sand one after another, the warm sea breeze blows across my face and in my hair before the humidity of the day hits. My lungs expand as I breathe in deep gulps of air. My feet take me as far as my lungs allow before I see a cliffside that blocks the path around to the other side of the island.

I stop running to analyze the rock face. *I wonder how far around it goes...* The more I think about it, the more I realize that it's the best thing to do. We need to hike up into the forest from here, then we'll be able to get on top of the cliff and see what we're dealing with on the other side.

"WE HAVE TO MOVE OUR CAMP," I say to the others as soon as I'm back. The men are all up, trying to get the fire going again. Lauren is awake too, but still lying next to Marcella, who's snoring softly.

"What did you see?" Wade asks.

"I didn't see anything. But the cliff—we should be closer to it. We can work on getting up over and around it. Who knows what we'll find on the other side."

"What about the water and food? We're already so far away from them... if anything, shouldn't we be moving closer to them, not farther away?" Caleb says.

I look at Graham, who normally has something smart-ass to add, but he's staying silent so far. "We can stock up a little today and move tomorrow," I say. "I can go back with Tom, and we can grab as many bananas as he can pick. Others can carry water. I really think getting to higher ground will be good, the cliffside can protect us if a storm comes our way—"

"We outran the storm," Lauren calls from where she's lying.

"It could still get to us eventually. Who knows which direction it was traveling? Or there could be another? It *is* hurricane season, after all. Remember the cheap tickets that *Andrew* hooked us up with?"

That shuts her up. She pinches her lips together, her face flames.

"We'd have to build another shelter," Wade says.

"We could try keeping part of this one, maybe carry it in sections or something. There might be more umbrellas and loungers over there."

"That's so much work if there's not," Lauren says, daring to speak again.

"Do you have something more important to do?" I can't hold back the snap in my voice. I'm starting to get so irritated with all the complaining, all the *can't, can't, can't,* it's like I'm the only one who wants to get out of this damn place.

"I wouldn't mind going back," Tom starts.

"Let's all calm down for a second," Caleb says, interrupting. "I see your point, Erin, but it's going to be a lot of work. Anyone up for a vote?" He looks around at the others.

"Let's wait for Marcella," Wade says.

"I'm up," she calls.

"How much did you hear?" he asks.

"I heard enough. And I think it's stupid."

I look from her to each of the others, and it's clear she's not the only one who feels that way. Graham still hasn't spoken. He's normally the first to say when something doesn't add up, so what's his problem now?

"Okay, that's a vote for no," Caleb says. "Tom, yay or nay?"

Tom looks at me, then around the group. "Can I stay neutral?" he asks. "I don't mind either way."

"We'll come back to you later then. Wade, what's your vote?"

"I don't think it's in our best interest to move," he says.

"Lauren?" Caleb asks.

"No."

"I'm going to have to vote no, too," he says. "Graham, you're up."

Graham frowns. "Erin's right. We need to get around that cliff. Who cares if it's *more work*? We're trying to get out of here, aren't we? What's wrong with all of you?"

I feel a pressure lift off my chest. *I'm not alone.*

"The calories we'd spend getting set up over there—" Caleb starts.

"Calories!" Graham barks. "We're talking about getting *off* this island, not making ourselves cozy!" He looks at Tom. "Tom, if you don't care one way or another if we get off this godforsaken place, your head is not in the right place, man."

Tom purses his lips. He nods. "I suppose—"

"No—you're not doing that," Marcella says, coming closer. "He's the only one who can climb a banana tree, and you're not taking him from us."

"No one is taking anyone from anyone," I say. "We're *all* doing this together."

"I'm not moving a foot down the beach," she says, crossing her arms.

I grind my teeth, wanting to throttle her. She looks at Wade. "Wade?"

"What?"

"Hey, I can think for myself, thanks very much," Tom says, giving Marcella an annoyed look. "I'll go with the majority," he says. "Whatever the vote turns out to be."

"Thank you!" Marcella says, throwing up her hands.

"Maybe we should split up," Lauren says.

"No—" I start.

"It might be for the best," Caleb says. *Of course he would agree with her.*

I look at him, dumbfounded. *They can't be serious.*

"That's a terrible idea," Graham says. "Are you crazy?"

"What's so crazy about it?" Lauren asks.

"For starters, there's safety in numbers. We can work as a team to get supplies, we'll be safer. When someone comes for us, we'll all be right there together."

"When?" Marcella laughs. "No one is coming."

"So we're just supposed to make ourselves at home and *die* here?" I cry. "Look at us! We *still* don't even have a fire. How do you expect us to survive?" I could almost pull my hair out at what I'm hearing. This is almost as bad as refusing to use the flare gun to get a fire started—which they still do.

Everyone is silent. I'm on pins and needles, waiting for someone to say something. The *right* thing to bring us together instead of breaking us further apart. I look to Wade, who's scowling, looking at his feet. He can't meet my eyes. *Say something, goddammit.*

"No one is going to make anyone else stay or go," Wade finally says. "If you think it's best to go, then go. If you want to stay, stay."

I meet Graham's gaze. He doesn't seem to be worried. I know I have to look scared enough for the both of us. "That's that, then," he says. *End of discussion.*

I swallow the lump in my throat. *Why do I feel like this is a harder decision than when I made up my mind to leave Matt?* "Tom," I say. "Will you come with us? There is no majority here."

"Um, two to four," Marcella says. "Last time I checked, those are not equal. Where the hell did you learn math?"

I glare at her. *What happened between us?* I wouldn't even be here if it wasn't for her. And since that day on the ship, she's been treating me more like her enemy than her best friend. I did nothing to deserve this treatment from her. I feel like I don't even know this person. She's a complete stranger to me.

"I'll go," Tom says.

I beam at him, relieved, thankful. I try not to cry, but tears threaten to spill anyway. "Thank you," I manage to say.

"Hang on!" Lauren cries.

"We'll go tomorrow," Graham says, ignoring her. "Today, we prepare. We need to gather food and water."

Tom and I both nod.

CHAPTER TWELVE

Six of us are back in the forest, trekking back to the food and water. Caleb stayed on the beach, just in case, by some miracle, someone comes to rescue us. It would be pretty crazy if someone came and we were all away.

I try not to be angry with the others—they're only doing what they think is best. But it's hard to not hold it against them for being so narrow minded. *Or is it laziness?* No—

"You don't have to leave," Wade says next to my ear, pulling me away from my own thoughts.

I take a step farther away from him. It rattles me that I didn't even notice him. He was ahead of the group a few minutes ago, and now he's next to me.

"It seems like I do."

"We don't have to separate."

"You're right. We don't, and we shouldn't." I give him a look that I hope conveys how stupid I think this all is.

"We can talk some more about it. There might be another way—"

"You all had your say. The discussion is over, I thought?"

Wade frowns. "It doesn't have to be like this."

"I don't *want* it to be like this. I want you all to see reason. If we don't at least see what's on the other side of that island, we're a bunch of idiots who deserve to die here. What if there's a fucking city over there?" I take a deep breath, trying to calm my temper.

Wade only says, "There's not."

I snort. "How do you know?"

"We would hear them."

I think about that. He could have a point there—it's so quiet on this island, we can probably head clear to the other side and not even know it. But that's the thing—we *don't* know. Not for sure, anyway.

"I have to see."

Wade purses his lips. "What if you and Graham took a few days to just check it out? Then you can come back and report what you see. You don't have to set up a new camp over there or whatever you're thinking. We can all still stick together as one group."

I stumble over a tree root, and he catches me before I fall on my face. We both stand there for a minute, contemplating, before continuing to walk. The others are farther ahead now, but Lauren's back is still visible.

"It might take longer than a couple of days," I finally say.

He nods. "However long it takes, then join us again."

"I mean—It's not like we're going to find a way out of here and not tell you guys. You don't think we would do that, do you?"

"That's not what I mean—"

"Hey, you guys okay back there?" Tom calls from ahead. Wade and I look to see him waiting for us at the top of a hill. We've been talking too much, moving too slow.

"Sorry," I call back to him, picking up my pace. To Wade, I say, "We'll talk about it later."

THE BANANA TREE is taller than I remember. *How is it so tall?* We all crane our necks to look up at the tree.

"Is there more up there?" Marcella asks Tom.

"Yeah. I didn't get them all."

"We're all going to have the shits," Graham says, halfway laughing.

"We'll find other food, but this is all we have for now. It's better than nothing," I say.

"There might be other trees nearby," Tom says. "I'll go look."

"Don't go far," Lauren calls after him. She hasn't let him out of her sight since he agreed to go with us.

We wait for a few minutes then Marcella says, "Why did we let our only tree climber take off? He could be climbing up there while one of us looks for more trees."

We let out a collective sigh as response. *She's right.* None of us are thinking clearly. It worries me that someone is going to make a dumb mistake.

"We should split up and go find water," I say. "Who's going to stay to help Tom?"

"I'll stay," Lauren says.

"Me too," Marcella adds.

"Okay, are you both with me then?" I ask Graham and Wade.

"We might be able to carry more bananas," Graham says. "We both have longer arms, can maybe hold more weight—"

"Don't be sexist," Marcella says. "Water is heavier than bananas anyway."

"Not with this amount," he says, holding up the clear backpacks full of the empty water bottles. "At this rate, you guys are going to have to go back and get water every day."

"What do you mean, *you guys?*" Marcella demands.

"Since we are leaving," Graham says slowly, pointing to me and to the forest where Tom stepped away. "We are taking our share of the water containers with us."

She scowls at him, her face turning beet red.

"*You guys* are going to have to figure something else out or be really, really thirsty," he continues with a mocking smile. He's giving Marcella a taste of her own medicine, and I have this sudden urge to kiss him. Her attitude has been grating on me since the moment we left the ship, and the look on her face now is priceless.

"You're not taking anything," Lauren says.

"Like hell we aren't," I say.

"If you guys want to leave, then leave. The supplies are for all of us, not just *you.*"

"*I* brought most of those water bottles with me, so maybe I should just take back *all* the ones that are *mine* if we're going to play that game."

"Hang on, hang on, everyone, just calm down a second," Wade says.

Graham is gripping the backpacks a little harder. *Good.* There's no way we're going to let them keep all the bottles. How can they not see the right thing to do is to split them evenly?

"They're already taking Tom. Now they want to take our water too—" Marcella growls.

"Aren't we supposed to be friends? What the hell is wrong with you?" I let it slip, unable to hold back anymore. I'm so angry with myself. They say people show their true colors in a life and death situation, and I'm seeing clearly that my *friend* isn't really my friend at all—no matter how long we've known each other. *How did I let her talk me into this situation?*

"Will everyone just listen a minute," Wade says. "We need to calm down, get the supplies, and get out of this forest. Can we all agree to argue back on the beach?"

Graham looks at me. "Let's get that water. Tom's got the bananas covered."

I nod.

"I'm not letting you go alone," Lauren says.

"Come with us then," Graham says.

"I'll go," Wade says. "You and Marcella stay and help Tom. Just like we talked about. We'll circle back around soon."

"What if Tom doesn't come back?" Lauren asks.

"He will. Just wait for him. Don't separate."

We move to leave. Marcella calls after us, "Don't let them steal our water, Wade."

Graham and I share a look and then lead the way to the water.

CHAPTER THIRTEEN

THE WATER IS JUST as cool and fresh as I remember. Kneeling on some large rocks, I dip my hands into the gurgling stream and slurp until my thirst is quenched. The water runs down my chin and neck, cooling my hot skin. I splash some more on myself, relishing the feeling.

Graham and Wade do the same farther downstream. There's a moment when I wonder why we don't just set up camp here, just like Caleb mentioned before. *It would save us so much trouble.* But it's obvious we can't. We would never know if someone came to save us, and we'd never know what's on the other side of the island.

"It's been seven days since we boarded the ship," I blurt out. A wave of fatigue hits me, pulling me down. The only thing we've had to eat—bananas and the meager snacks that are long gone—hasn't been enough. Not even close.

The others don't answer. It's a shock to all of us that we're still here. We should be getting ready to leave the cruise ship, say our goodbyes, and go home, not be looking for a way to survive.

As we're bent, filling the rest of the bottles, a scream fills the air. Wade stands up, a panicked look on his face. "Did you hear that?"

Graham looks skeptical. "Yeah, I heard."

"We need to go back."

"No, we need to finish getting water. There're only a few more bottles."

"Someone could be hurt," Wade insists.

"You can go check on them. I'll help Graham finish here," I offer. He looks like he might agree but stops short. He eyes Graham carefully, then the bottles.

My face burns. "You don't really think we're going to run off with the water, do you?"

Wade's jaw clenches. "No. I don't think you would." It's obvious he doesn't think so highly of Graham though. I can't really blame him, I wouldn't have put it past him a couple of days ago either, but things are different now. He might be an ass sometimes, but I know he wouldn't pull something like that.

"By the time we're done arguing, we could've been long done and gone," Graham drones.

Wade pauses, then nods. "Right. Let's hurry."

The flow of water is slower than we'd like, but fast enough to give us what we need. It doesn't take much longer to finish filling the plastic backpacks and the rest of the bottles, and by the time we're done, we all have our hands full.

"Do you think one of them is hurt?" I ask Graham as we head back into the forest, Wade leading the way.

He shrugs. "Maybe. I haven't heard another scream, have you?"

I shake my head. "No."

"Might be they saw a giant bug or something."

"I hope so."

AS WE GET CLOSER, we begin to hear more sounds, muffled talking, and what sounds like crying. I scan the trees, trying to get a better view of what's going on, but they're still too far. "Should we call to them?"

"No. You might startle Tom," Graham says.

We pick up our pace. When we're close enough for them to hear our footsteps, Lauren calls. "Is that you guys?"

"It's us. Is everyone okay?" Wade yells to her.

"No." The word comes as more of a strangled choking sound than anything else. Wade breaks into a sprint, Graham and I do too, none of us thinking about how thirsty we're going to be after running.

Wade reaches them first, followed by Graham. "Fuck!" Graham yells. Wade turns around and holds me back from seeing. He looks down at me with a look so frightened I can only think one thing. *Someone is hurt.*

"I'm not a child, Wade. I want to see what's happening."

"It's bad," he says low, shaking his head. "You don't want to see this."

"I'm not a child," I say again, clenching my fists. He's acting so much like my ex-husband right now, I have to hold myself back from screaming at him. This is exactly something Matt would pull, trying to shield me.

Wade finally takes a step back. Everyone is looking at something on the ground. I take a few steps forward, trying to see what they see. Then I do.

I hold my hands over my mouth. *It's Tom.* He's—dead.

He's lying faceup, mouth wide like he was screaming

before he fell. His head is caved in, in the back, brain matter splattered on the ground beside him. One of Tom's legs is bent beneath his body, the other twisted at an unnatural angle.

Wade vomits as Graham inspects Tom's body. Lauren is standing back, wringing her hands together, sobbing. "Where's Marcella?" I choke.

My voice comes out as something I don't recognize—raspy and used up. The world is spinning. *This can't be happening.*

"She went to find you," Lauren says.

"When did he fall?"

"I don't know! I don't have a fucking clock!" she screams.

I wipe tears away from my own eyes. *Poor Tom.* He didn't deserve this.

A rustling comes from nearby and Marcella steps out panting, her eyes red rimmed and cheeks tearstained. "Where the hell were you?" she demands, looking straight at me.

"We heard someone scream," Wade says. "We came as soon as we could."

"He needed you!" she says. "*We* needed you."

"What were we supposed to do? Fly over here?" Graham says. "Let's not place blame on the people who weren't even here."

"What happened?" Wade says.

Marcella won't stop staring at me. She grinds her teeth and wipes at her face. Finally she looks at Wade, and says, "Isn't it obvious? He fucking fell."

CHAPTER FOURTEEN

WE HAVE no way to bury Tom, but we can't just leave him there either. Wade and Graham carry his body while the rest of us hold the other supplies. There are a few bananas—not enough. None of us mentions it.

There's nothing to say. We walk in silence, listening to the waves in the distance and the sound of our own racing hearts. By the time we get back, the sun is setting, and we're all done in.

Lauren falls into Caleb's arms the moment he's within sight. "What the hell happened?" he asks. Then he sees Tom and his face drains of color.

"There was a terrible accident," Lauren says.

Wade and Graham set Tom's body near the edge of the forest. "Won't animals get him?" Marcella asks.

"We'll keep watch," Wade says.

"We could dig a shallow grave," I say.

"Using what?" she asks.

I throw my arms up at her tone. "Then what do you suggest? Why even ask about it if there's nothing we can do for him?"

"We can set him out to sea," Graham says.

"Will he make it out there or just float back?" Marcella asks, the same defiance in her voice.

"Do we have permission to use the flare gun now, majesties?" I look between Wade and Graham, daring them to come up with another excuse.

A look passed between them. Wade says, "I thought we agreed to shoot it when there's a sign of someone nearby."

"No. *You both* said if we have a death on our hands, it would change things."

"I just don't see the point in shooting it if there's no one around to see."

My jaw is clenched so hard, my teeth are protesting. I look toward Graham, and it's clear he's not going to speak up to agree with me on this. No one else will either—they're still reeling over our loss of Tom.

"Don't you think we should worry about Tom first?" Marcella sneers. "Thanks for being so insensitive."

They go back to discussing Tom, no further mention of the flare gun. I've had about enough of Marcella as I can take, so I walk away. *Let them deal with it.* I'm sure Tom wouldn't care anyway.

We can barely stand each other already. How are things going to be after *months*? *Years*? I shudder at the thought. We have to try harder.

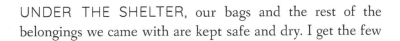

UNDER THE SHELTER, our bags and the rest of the belongings we came with are kept safe and dry. I get the few possessions I have and set them outside, ready to leave for the morning. I'm not sure when I'll be coming back.

I know it's the right thing to do. I'm not going to die here. Not like Tom. I'm not going to just sit here and get comfortable and wait for it to be over—just like my marriage. *I won't do it again.*

When I'm finished gathering my things, I go to find Graham to tell him he should do the same. I walk to the far side of the beach looking for him when I hear whispered voices. "It's all my fault," a woman cries.

I know I should step away, give them privacy, but part of me wants to know what *really* happened. There has to be more that Lauren and Marcella didn't say.

"It's not. Don't even think that," a voice says.

I take a step closer, staying low so I'm out of sight.

"I'm the one who—who said—" Lauren breaks down in tears.

"It doesn't matter what you said. You didn't *do* anything," Caleb says.

"I should have! I should have stopped it!"

Stopped what? My eyes are growing wider by the second. A cold sweat breaks out on my forehead, and suddenly I don't want to wait until tomorrow to get out of here. I want to find Graham so we can leave *now.*

"There was nothing you could do," Caleb reassures her.

More crying comes, followed by some sniffles. "If he would've just agreed to stay with us—"

A pause. "It's done now. Everything is going to be okay."

"How? They're going to take half of our water with them. We'll have to—"

I lean too far, and a small branch cracks beneath my palm. I hold my breath when Lauren stops talking. *Please, please, please!*

"Everything's going to be fine. Trust me," Caleb says again.

I release a small sigh. They stop talking altogether now and make other sounds that tell me the conversation is over. I move away from them, desperate to find Graham.

WHERE IS HE, *where is he?* When I'm far enough away from Caleb and Lauren, I start to call for him. At the same time, my mind is spinning with what I've overheard. *Tom's fall was no accident.*

Lauren and Marcella both knew, *obviously*, and now Caleb... does Wade know? Does he suspect?

I think about telling him too. He has a right to know—I can't leave him with these people, not knowing what they're capable of. What *Marcella* is capable of.

As I'm wiping away tears, I stumble into Wade. My head knocks into his chin. "I'm so sorry," I say.

We steady ourselves. "What's wrong?" he asks.

I'm about to tell him everything I've learned but Graham steps out. "Were you calling for me?"

I've never been so happy to see him. I sigh, overwhelmed with relief. "Yes. I—" I glance between him and Wade. "I have all my stuff together; I think you should do the same so we can go."

"You're still leaving? Even after—" Wade says.

"Don't you see we have to? If we can get over to the other side of that cliff—maybe—"

"Maybe what? A city full of people is waiting, ready to welcome us with open arms?"

There's something in his tone, in the reflection of his eyes, that gives me pause. A sinking feeling grows in the pit of my stomach. *He's starting to sound a lot like Marcella.*

I look to Graham, whose lips are pressed into a fine line. "I'm ready when you are," he says with a knowing look. The moment to tell Wade passes. I let it go, not sure he'll even believe me if I tried.

I nod. I look at the sky. "It's getting dark. We can leave at first light." I hope Graham can read the look I'm trying to give him that says the opposite. *We need to get the hell out of here.*

CHAPTER FIFTEEN

When I open my eyes, Graham is staring at me. It's pitch black now, but I can still see his eyebrows rise in question. I nod.

Slowly, he gets up first, giving me more room to get out from under Wade's arm. I hold my breath when his breathing changes. I wait, praying he won't wake up. The sudden loss of body heat in the cold night air is probably going to wake him eventually—I just hope we're well on our way before it does.

Graham grabs both our packs and motions for me to hurry. I wait for him to take a few steps away before finally following.

Every step we take, I'm terrified of someone waking and calling out to us. If Marcella and Lauren are capable of killing Tom for wanting to go with us, who knows what they'll be willing to do to stop us from—

"Where's the water?" Graham whispers. He searches frantically, everywhere he can think of, but the bottles are gone.

"I don't know. I thought they were there." I point to where

we've been working on building a fire, the place we've been dropping all resources.

"It was here last night." He runs his hands through his hair. "They did something with it. They didn't want us to have any."

A day ago, I would've argued. I would've never believed Marcella or the others would be capable of doing something so *cruel*. Now though, I wouldn't put it past her—or them. "What are we going to do?"

It's hard to see his face in the low light, but it's clear how pissed he is. "We'll take another look around. Look everywhere. Then, we leave—with or without the water."

"Are you sure? We can wait?"

He doesn't speak. His footsteps away are answer enough. *We're going tonight, one way or another.*

I LOOK BACK under the shelter. The water could be *between* Marcella and Caleb or Wade for all we know. I wouldn't doubt she would try something like that.

I tiptoe past their feet, trying to see any sign of the water in the dark. There are quite a few bottles, and the backpacks— if we even found a couple, it would be better than nothing. I'm already growing thirsty just thinking about it.

There's nothing here. I leave, searching around the best I can, then heading for the tree line. Maybe the water is hidden farther away.

Graham meets me with the same thought. "Any luck?"

"No."

"Me either." He clenches his fists. "I checked the trees—

nothing there either, unless they went farther in. There's no way to know."

"Should we wait until daylight? We'll see better—"

"No." Graham shakes his head. "This is dirty, Erin. Dirty as hell."

"I know it is."

"If they're playing this low, I don't even want to think about what else they're capable of."

"Tom's fall wasn't an accident." I blurt it out, knowing it's not the best time, but I have to tell him. We have to be on the same page if we're going to work together.

Graham sucks in a breath. "Are you sure?"

"Yes. I'll tell you everything."

"Later. When we get the hell out of here."

"Yes."

"Fuck!" he breathes, running his hands through his hair. He sighs. "The longer we spend looking for the water, the more of a chance there is that we'll wake someone. I don't think we should stay much longer. What do you think?"

Despite everything, I smile at him. He's not telling me how it's going to be or telling me what we're going to do. He's asking. And he really cares what I have to say about it.

It's so different from the way I've been treated for as long as I can remember. Not just with Matt but with most people in my life. It's something so small, insignificant really in the scheme of things, especially in the situation we're in, but it still means so much.

"This isn't really something to smile about," Graham says.

"I think you're right—about leaving now. Let's just go and hope for the best. Were you able to grab any bananas?"

"Luckily, I thought to hide some of those in my pack yesterday." He pats his bag. "I think they hid the rest along with the water."

I clench my jaw. "Okay. Let's get out of here."

We set out but only make it about a hundred feet before a voice calls to us. "Erin?"

I turn to see Wade standing outside the shelter. I look back at Graham. "Should we ask him about the water?"

"Maybe. But let's be quick. I don't want to wake the others."

We take a few steps toward Wade and wait for him to come to us. "Where's the water?" Graham demands, cutting straight to it.

"Why are you leaving now? I thought you were going in the morning."

"Answer him," I say. "Where's the water, Wade?"

His eyebrows furrow. "In the same place we left it last night. I don't know what you're talking about."

"It's not there. Someone did something with it so we wouldn't be able to take any."

"If you know where it is, help us," Graham says.

Wade shakes his head. "I don't. No one told me anything. I'm—sorry."

I glance from Wade to Graham and back again, weighing our choices. "Come with us," I say.

He looks surprised that I would ask. "I don't think it's a good idea to separate."

"We're separating no matter what."

Wade looks to Graham, who stays silent. They stare at each other for a moment, unmoving, each looking as if he was reading the other's thoughts.

"We have to go," I say. "Will you come with us or not?"

"No."

"Come on," Graham says to me. "Let's get out of here."

"If we find anything, we'll tell you," I say.

Wade nods and Graham and I turn to go.

CHAPTER SIXTEEN

THE FEW TIMES I've gone jogging down the beach, I've been going for about an hour, then turning around and jogging back. I went to have the time to myself, to clear my head, rather than for the distance. The sand slowed me down, but it didn't matter because I wasn't thinking about speed or distance, I was thinking about anything other than being stuck here.

Today is different. Graham and I are thinking about distance and the fact that we don't have any water. We're also thinking about getting the hell away from the others as fast as we can. We decide to make it all the way to the front of the rock face before stopping, and it takes us hours, going as slow as we can to prevent our thirst from growing but steadily without breaks. The entire time, a clawing sensation is on the back of my neck, telling me we're going to end up just like Tom.

"Do you think they'll come after us?" I ask Graham when we stop for the day.

"They have no reason to."

"They had no reason to kill Tom, either."

Graham's lips press into a thin line. "Tell me what you know."

I tell him about the conversation I overheard between Caleb and Lauren, and a dark look passes over his face, along with something that looks like fear. He believes Marcella and Lauren had something to do with Tom's fall too.

"I don't understand why they were that worried," I say. "We could have figured something out without them *killing* him. We could share the water too—figure something out for all of us. What the hell is wrong with them?"

"They're not seeing reason. They're too afraid." The sun is starting to come up on the horizon. Graham picks a spot to sit and watch it.

I sit next to him and use my pack as a pillow to lay my head on. "What are we going to do about water?"

"We'll be fine for today. Tomorrow, if we still haven't found any." He shrugs. "We'll have to go back and get some."

"It will take all day to go there and back again, and what if—"

"Listen, let's not think about it. It's only going to stress us out. Let's worry about getting some food and shelter, and dare I say it—a fire."

We're silent as the sun rises the rest of the way into the sky. Before long, Graham's soft snoring is all I hear. I find myself falling asleep soon after.

"ERIN, WAKE UP!" Graham shakes me awake full of eager excitement.

"What is it?"

"Water!"

I sit up. "Where?"

"Someone left it for us—one of the clear backpacks filled to the brim." He holds up the bag for me to see. It's so beautiful I could almost weep.

"Was it Wade?"

Graham shakes his head. "I don't know. I was looking around, backtracked a ways trying to peek into the forest to see what's around, and I came across it sitting in the sand."

He grins at me, and I return the smile. Carefully, we take turns sipping the water. There's enough to last us a couple of days if we ration it.

I think about when I heard noises at night, the animal whose eyes were on me. What if it wasn't an animal after all? What if it was Wade or one of the others watching me? I shiver, glad to be here with Graham now, but suddenly worried that we're not far enough away yet.

"So, do we keep going now?"

Graham looks at the sky, gauging what time it might be. "It might be dangerous camping in the forest. We don't know how long it will take to make our way over to the other side of the cliff. Do you feel like walking the rest of the day?"

I nod. "Yes. It's why we're here, right?" The idea of being a little more hidden beneath the trees sits well with me. Sure, they brought us water, but what if they're not so friendly next time? After what happened with Tom, I'm not sure who I'm willing to trust.

He nods back. "OK then. Let's get moving."

Graham slips his pack on his back and the clear bag full of water onto his chest. I could almost laugh at how careful he's being with it, if it wasn't filled with such a precious commodity.

We head back down the beach in the direction we came, then as soon as the land levels out enough, we climb up into the forest, heading back toward the top of the cliff. We stay near the edge of the tree line, so the bluff is visible and we'll know where to descend.

CHAPTER SEVENTEEN

We haven't been able to find a clear path through, even after spending nearly the entire day trying. The sky is turning dark now, as it seems one of our worst fears is about to come true. A storm. I look at Graham, trying to contain my fear. "What should we do?"

We both realize how stupid we've been. We should've focused on the shelter first. *That always comes first.* We were too worried about getting over to the other side, too worried about water, about everything else. Now it's going to bite us in the ass.

Graham grimaces. "It's moving in quick. We need to make whatever shelter we can while we have the chance. If we get up next to the side of the cliff, it might help shelter us from some of it."

It's a good idea. The only problem is that we'll have to go back to the beach—an entire day lost. We'll also have to drag branches and leaves farther. There are no tiki umbrellas or lounge chairs to use here. We'll have to start from scratch. It'll take longer and require more effort but might have a bigger payout. *Maybe.*

We decide it'll be better than camping out in the forest, where trees might fall on us or who knows what might come upon us. Better to stay on the beach and try for a shelter. There's not much time, but we don't really have a choice. If we get pneumonia out here, we will die. There's no question.

Graham and I get to work, dragging as much as we can at a time. The wind picks up. When we have a pile started, we start to lean the biggest branches up to make the start of our shelter. I lose my grip on a handful of palm leaves and they fly down the beach, along the rock face, closer to the water's edge.

"Shit!" I run after them.

"Leave them," Graham calls, struggling with his own part of the shelter.

I ignore him, too frustrated to lose them. Everything keeps falling down on me, and I feel useless. The least I could do is go after them when they're not too far away yet—before we have to go and get more.

"I'll just be a sec," I yell, running toward the water. The stack separates, but they're all blowing in the same direction, almost right up against the huge wall of rock. Rain starts drizzling down. *We're running out of time.*

I look back to see Graham continuing to build the shelter. It's so small and weak, I'm not sure how it's going to hold up if the wind gets any stronger.

The palm leaves are within reach. I grab one and then another. The rest of them jump with the breeze and flop on top of the water. *Only one or two steps out.* I rush to get them before the waves carry them out.

I cry out as I trip on something under the water. I throw my arms out, trying to catch myself as I fall, but I land hard, breathing in water in my struggle. I cough, fighting to get air into my lungs.

Graham's footsteps draw nearer. He's running to me. "I'm here, it's okay." He pounds my back, urging me to cough up the water.

I gasp in a breath. "I'm sorry." Tears spring to my eyes when I see it's all been for nothing. I let go of the stupid leaves in my fall—now I have nothing.

"It was an accident. You're okay now. We're going to be okay."

His kindness makes me want to cry even more. Graham isn't *kind*. He's real. And if he's being kind—he's not being real.

He helps me up and out of the water. We take a second on the sand to stop and assess if I'm too badly damaged. As we do, Graham stops and stares at something behind me. "Am I going crazy? Tell me you see that too."

I turn to see what he's squinting at. "What is it?" My pulse quickens. "Is it the ship?"

He points at the rock face, shaking his head. "No. It looks like—" He takes a few steps forward and tilts his head trying to see better.

"You're scaring me! What is it?"

"It looks like an opening. A cave, maybe."

A *cave?* "I don't see it," I say carefully. "But a cave doesn't matter, right?"

He looks at me now. "Hell yes, it matters. That's shelter, Erin."

"But—what if there's something living in there? We have no light, no fire—" I raise my eyebrows in reference to the flare gun. Without saying the word he knows what I want.

Graham doesn't acknowledge the unspoken request. He says, "There's nothing living in there. You'd have to swim to get to it unless it was low tide. Would you rather get soaked under some palm leaves and maybe catch hypothermia while you're at it?"

"I wouldn't catch hypothermia if we used the flare gun to start a fire..."

"Please, Erin. We're running out of time before the storm hits."

I bite my lip and look out at the water. "I'm afraid."

"It's okay," he says, softening. "We'll go together. It's not far."

"Will there be sharks?"

"Maybe. But I think I heard somewhere they go less active during storms, swim to deeper waters."

I can't tell if he's making it up or not. He's an author—making shit up is what he does. I sigh, knowing it doesn't matter. Graham is right. If there's a cave, it's our best chance at shelter.

The sky opens. *Time's up.* I look at our halfway-falling palm shelter and choke back a sob. "What if it isn't a cave? What if it's nothing?"

"I'm willing to risk it," he says. "Are you?"

I nod and reach for his hand. "Let's go."

CHAPTER EIGHTEEN

THE WATER IS warm against the pelting rain. Graham holds my hand as we start for the cave, leaving everything else behind. "We can go back for it when the storm's over," he says.

"The water—"

"It will be fine. It's safe."

I hope he's right. I think about my laptop and what little supplies we have left out in the rain. We won't be able to carry them through the water, not if we want to make it into the cave, but it stings to leave them behind. What if something happens to me? Will anyone ever find my words?

"Can we at least take the flare gun with us?"

"*That* again?" He raises his eyebrows.

"I promise I won't fight you on it. Not right now anyway—I just feel better having it near us. Just in case."

Graham indulges me by unpacking the cartridges and gun and stuffing them into his pockets. Even if we're not starting a fire, at least I know we won't be caught with our pants down if a ship does decide to show up.

He pulls me forward through the water. Even with all the

jogging I do, he's still a far better swimmer. My head hurts from when I fell. It makes me somewhat disoriented, but he keeps me on track, keeps me from falling below the surface.

"Almost there," he pants.

I find myself trusting him, despite all the betrayal I've faced in the last week and the nightmare situation we find ourselves in, I lean on him and allow him to help me, to guide me toward our shelter.

Something brushes against my leg. I still, terrified of what it might be. "Graham," I whisper. My hand slips from him.

He keeps going, unable to hear, not noticing that I've stopped.

"Graham!" I say louder.

"What's wrong?"

"Something brushed against my leg." I pull myself closer to him, wanting to kick harder, get to the cave faster, but knowing that kicking legs underwater is only going to draw a predator nearer.

"It's okay," Graham says. He looks at the rock face and then gives me a reassuring smile. "It's definitely a cave, look."

As I look, Graham continues to swim, pulling us both forward. I'm torn between fear and relief already, and now guilt. He's willing to risk his own legs to get us to where we need to be.

"Should we stop kicking?" I ask.

"We'll never get there if we don't."

"But if it's a—"

"It's not. It's just a fish. Or seaweed." He keeps going. We're so close now, I can see the opening of the cave clearly. Hope rises, making my eyes water. *We're going to make it.*

I renew my efforts, kicking faster than before. Our speed increases. When I look up again, we're just below the entrance. I look up at the rock, wet with rain and ocean spray.

Even if it wasn't so slippery, there's still barely a ledge to hold on to.

"How do we get in?" I turn to Graham with wide eyes, afraid of what comes next.

"We have to pull ourselves up."

"I don't think I'm that strong," I choke.

"It's okay. I'll go first and pull you up after." He gives me a reassuring smile, nothing but confidence radiating through his eyes.

We look for something sticking out, anything that might allow him to get a good grip. The entrance looks small but big enough for me to stand up in. Graham might have to bend a little to get in.

"I think I found something," Graham calls. He reaches up to grab a large rock that's protruding. His fingers bend at an odd angle, trying to get a good grip.

"Don't force it," I say.

"It's okay. I have it—" With effort, he pulls himself up and out of the water, hanging to the side of the bluff by a single rock.

I cringe, feeling helpless when his feet start to slip. Something catches my eye. "Put your foot to the right!"

Graham listens without even trying to look, and his foot finds just enough of a ledge to hold some weight. He's close enough now where he can reach his arm out and grab the inside of the cave opening. If he can get a good enough grip, he can pull himself right inside.

I'm treading water, looking up at him struggling. The rain is still coming in torrents. Graham slips more than once on the wet rocks. I make sure to stay far enough back that if he falls, he won't land on me.

I wish there was something I could say, something I could do to help. I analyze the rock face again, deciding to at least make the effort to try pulling myself up. It won't hurt to give it a shot.

I reach for a small rock that's sticking out, about an arm's length away from Graham. It's too high. I try to reach for it again. I scrape against the wall on my way back down into the water, crying out as my face is skinned.

Graham looks at me, distracted. "Are you okay?"

"Fine. Just trying to make myself useful."

"Don't kill yourself in the process, okay?"

"I'll try," I huff. *That's enough of that.* I tread back out a little, away from the rocks.

I freeze. Something brushes against my leg again. "Graham."

"Erin, I got it. I'm in."

"Graham," I say again, trying not to panic.

He looks at me. Then I'm pulled under the water.

CHAPTER NINETEEN

My mouth and lungs fill with water as I go down. My limbs seize. I'm filled with panic all the way down to my core. I *know* I need to move, to get away, to do something—*anything*, but I'm frozen like a deer in the headlights.

I have a soul-deep urge to cough the water out, to inhale oxygen. I can feel the pressure building in my lungs, my face, my eyes. *Don't panic, Erin! Too late!*

Something is coming at me. I finally kick as hard as I can. My arms whip through the water, pulling me back to the surface. When I'm above it, I choke and cough and gasp for air.

"Erin!" Graham is calling. He stands at the edge of the cave opening, looking just as panicked as I feel.

"Graham!"

"You can make it!" He reaches out an arm.

I swim for him, but something brushes past me again. I choke back a sob. Something bites me, and I scream so loud I can feel my eardrums vibrating.

"Erin!" Graham yells again.

I kick and flail automatically, desperate to get away from

whatever's attacking me, to reach Graham. I suck in another breath, swallowing a mouthful of water in the process, and it hits me that I'm not in as much pain as I thought. *Shouldn't a shark bite hurt more than this?*

Adrenaline and hope surge through my veins. There's nothing holding me back except for the waves. I fight through them and the rain, reaching my hand out for Graham. He grasps me and pulls me up to him.

I cling to him, coughing up water, sobbing with relief. He sucks in a breath. "What the hell?"

"What is it?"

He grabs on to something that's attached itself to my back. I haven't even noticed it until Graham touches it, and it wiggles in protest.

"Grab it!" I scream. "Get it off me!" I dip as dizziness sets in, but I hang on, breathing in deep, steady breaths, willing it to pass.

Graham yanks and whatever was holding on to me lets go. "You can look now." He's holding up a slender gray *fish* that's about two feet long. "It's a Remora," he says. "It's like a sucker fish."

"Get that thing the hell away from me."

Graham throws the Remora back into the water. He bends down to look at my back. "Does it hurt?"

"A little. I think it scared the shit out of me more than anything." I feel like I could die from mortification. *A damn fish!* I thought I was going to be eaten alive by a shark and it was a damn suckerfish on my back. My heart rate still hasn't slowed to normal.

"Good," he says, trying not to laugh. "Now let's go in this cave and get dry, shall we?" he takes my hand and helps me to my feet. I'm glad this is something we can laugh about now because two minutes ago, I wasn't so sure.

Cautiously, we take a few steps inside the cave. The narrow path funnels into a wide-open area. "Do you think there are bats?" I whisper.

"It's a good possibility," Graham whispers back.

We both look up, but it's too dark to see. We stay next to each other, as quiet as possible so we don't startle any creatures that might be lurking. The waves lap past the entrance, affording us a little sound.

"Now what?"

Graham tugs me closer. He bends down to whisper closer to my ear. "Now we get warm."

Blood rushes to my face. "Is it safe?"

He laughs. "I just meant we need to get our wet clothes off. Get your mind out of the gutter, Erin."

My face heats further. I'm embarrassed because he's right. I know what he was thinking. He can't fool me. *But that's what I was thinking too.* These past nights of sleeping next to him, his body pressed against mine, the memories of Matt that come rushing in, *the loneliness*—it's tempting. *And he just saved my life...*

I take a step away from him, sober. He stops me before I get too far. "Hey."

"What?"

"You don't have to do anything you don't want to do."

I can feel his eyes on me even if I can't see them. I swallow at his change in tone. "I could say the same to you."

He comes closer. I flinch when his fingers touch my still-wet skin. "I do have a rain check to cash in..."

Gooseflesh breaks out on my arms. *How long has it been?* He reaches to brush the hair from my face. Then he kisses me.

CHAPTER TWENTY

I wake up in Graham's arms. Sunlight shines through the cave opening and it seems the waves have calmed. The storm has passed. I get up to peek outside and gasp at what I see. *It's low tide.*

I rush to wake Graham. "Graham, we have to go."

"What's wrong?" he asks, wiping sleep from his eyes.

"It's low tide. We can get back, but we have to go now."

He stands and goes to look, then grins at me. "Are you sure you wouldn't rather stay here for the day?"

I smile at him, blushing. "I would like to pee without you watching, if you don't mind."

He laughs. "Let's get going."

I can't help but be glad Graham isn't the asshole I originally thought he was. I like this side of him much better than the one I met on the cruise, and I find myself glad to be here with him. If I'm going to be stranded on an island with someone, I'm glad it's him.

He lowers me down into the water—not nearly as deep as yesterday. It's so shallow, my feet are probably less than a foot from touching the bottom. When Graham climbs down, he's able to walk.

When we make it to shore, we lie on the sand for a moment catching our breath. The storm from yesterday wreaked havoc on the island. Branches are everywhere. If we would've stayed—it would've been bad.

"Do you remember where we left the bags?" I ask, getting up.

"Over there," he points.

I'm forced to climb over tree limbs and move countless branches out of the way to make my way across the beach. Graham joins me in my search.

"I don't see them," I say, worry slowly working its way in.

"They're here somewhere," he says. "I'll look over there, you stay here."

We spread out our efforts, and after twenty minutes of still not seeing our supplies, we're both starting to have doubts. "The bags wouldn't fly away. They're too heavy," Graham says.

"I mean... the wind was pretty strong—"

"Not strong enough for that."

"There are fallen trees..."

He gives me a look.

"Okay, well what do you suggest?"

"I think we should keep looking. Without that water, we're going to be in trouble quick, not to mention the rest of our supplies. Thank God I have the flare gun."

I frown, not wanting to argue but also not agreeing completely. If we waste our time and effort looking when it's already long gone, I think we'll only be worse off. "Do you really think it's worth the effort?"

Graham frowns back at me. "Are you so sure it's not here?"

"I mean, we've been looking. Why wouldn't we have found it by now?"

We both look around. There are a lot of places the bags could be still, tons of spots where they'd be blocked from our view. But why would the bags be anywhere else? We were building *here*. *This* is where they were, where they would be.

He sighs. "Let's look for a little longer. If we don't find anything within another thirty minutes, we'll move on to plan B. How does that sound?"

I nod. "Agreed."

THIRTY MINUTES LATER, we're facing each other empty-handed. "Someone has to have taken them," Graham says.

"What? You really think they would do that?" I bite my tongue at my own words. They killed Tom. *What wouldn't they do* is more the question I should be asking.

"Maybe one of them found out about the water. They wanted to come back and take what was *theirs*."

I can see Marcella doing something like that. If she's capable of making Tom fall, there's no question. "Do you think they hurt Wade?"

"If he's the one who helped us... they might want to make sure he doesn't do it again." Graham looks like he wants to say more at the mention of Wade. He hasn't asked if there was anything between us—and there's not—but I also don't think he would've missed the looks between us. I'm not sure if he even cares, but I feel like I should say something.

"There was nothing between us, you know."

"It's none of my business."

"I just want you to know, that's all."

He smiles. "I know."

I purse my lips, already feeling the dryness of my mouth. "We don't know if that's what happened—one of them coming to take our stuff. Assuming it is though, what do we do now?"

Graham paces. "They would know we weren't here, but not where we were—"

"Unless they heard us." I color.

He grins. "I don't think they would've. Not from here."

"OK, so they don't know about the cave."

He nods. "Right. And they don't know where we are."

"Do we really think they would've gone out in the storm? Just to take our water and what little supplies we have?" I throw up my arms. "I feel like we're going to feel really stupid when we stumble across one of these backpacks."

"All I'm saying is—I wouldn't put it past them. We haven't found the bags, so..." He shrugs. "We just need to be prepared for a worst-case scenario."

"Worst-case scenario? As in what? Them—attacking us?" I can't believe what I'm hearing.

Graham presses his lips together and nods. "Yes."

"I can't believe this. They were only worried about their resources. If we leave them alone, they'll leave us alone. They're not going to *attack us*."

"Erin, we *were* leaving them alone." He stares at me until I look away. I'm starting to feel sick to my stomach.

"Fine," I say. "Assuming they went out in the storm, took our bags, and are now scoping us out, now what? What do we do?"

CHAPTER TWENTY-ONE

WE HAVE TO FIND WATER. Graham and I both realize now how stupid we were to not collect the rainwater from the storm, but too little too late. How were we supposed to know we wouldn't have water the next day? We are so *bad* at this survival crap. Part of me wonders what I was even thinking, coming over to this side of the island, actually believing I could make it around the cliff.

"We have today," Graham says. "We'll be fine without drinking something. But tomorrow." He grimaces. "Tomorrow we'll be feeling it."

"Let's get moving then."

We make our way up into the forest just like before, this time going farther inland instead of hugging the tree line. When Graham hears my stomach growling, he says, "You know, my last book involved people slowly starving to death."

"Oh yeah? Did you make them suffer?"

He grins. "I let one of them survive."

"So that means you know all about how to *not* die of starvation, right?"

"If I was writing us into a novel, sure."

I groan, "I know."

Graham nudges me. "Hey, we're creatives. We can figure something out."

I give him a grateful smile. We continue our uphill trek. I'm weaker than I've ever been. All I want to do is sleep, but I force myself to follow his footsteps, one foot after the next. My mind drifts in and out, focusing is a struggle. At one point, I catch myself and realize I haven't been paying full attention to our surroundings.

"Hang on a second," I call to Graham.

He stops. "Everything okay?"

"Have you been looking up?" I've been looking at the ground, trying not to lose my footing, when I should be looking up. If there's fruit—it's going to be growing up in the trees.

"Of course I have, haven't you?"

My face heats but thankfully he's not looking at me anymore. "Yeah, just making sure." Somehow I manage to look both up *and* down without tripping on too many tree roots or fallen branches. I'm starting to lose hope of finding food at all.

"Maybe our best shot is to catch some crabs at the beach. We don't need a fire if we catch one."

"We should try that too, but it could take us days to catch one."

It could take us days out here, too. I keep the words inside. I know being negative doesn't help anything, especially when we're trying our best. We both are. Why should I make him feel like shit for that?

AS THE DAY WEARS ON, the trees keep us shaded from the sun, but nothing satisfies our thirst. Graham licks the morning dew off some leaves, getting a few precious drops of moisture before it evaporates. I follow his example, but it does nothing except intensify the craving.

My mind wanders in circles, every thought revolving around water. Memories of Matt and I in the shower, in the pool, at the lake, on the boat—*water, water, water.*

I hear a noise that faintly sounds like a waterfall. I know it's my brain playing tricks on me. I ignore it. *If it's real, it'll get louder as we get closer.*

I pay attention, the noise never completely going away. It stops for a while and then—*there it is again.* It's familiar—a shuffling of the forest floor. My eyes widen as I realize what it is. I turn to Graham and hiss, "That's the same noise as before!"

My excitement is contagious, but he doesn't know what I'm talking about. "Before when?" he asks.

"The bananas!"

"There wasn't—"

"There were little birds, Graham! The birds!"

His eyes widen with recognition. He remembers now—the little birds that Caleb thought would be a waste of energy to hunt down. He grins at me. "The birds."

I grin back because it looks like we're finally going to have something to eat.

When we see the birds, I could almost scream from happiness. They're eating fruit alright, and it's not bananas.

Mangos. The ground is littered with them, and the birds are feasting. "They must've fallen in the storm," Graham says.

"Should we try for the birds?"

"We don't have a fire..." We look at each other for a moment, contemplating the cost of eating raw bird meat with the cost of letting the meat go. We're practically starving. The only food in days has been bananas. Any kind of meat sounds like heaven, but if we make ourselves sick—is it worth it?

"Let's stick with the fruit," I say.

Graham nods his agreement and sets off to scare the birds away. When they're gone, we dive in, brushing off anything that looks questionable and filling ourselves with the juicy flesh of the fruit. We stay until the sun starts to go down, reluctant to leave the paradise within the trees.

CHAPTER TWENTY-TWO

IT'S BEEN TOO many days since we've had an actual meal. The fruit takes like heaven, but my stomach still protests constantly. I've never known true hunger before this. Now, I can almost laugh at my ignorance.

Biting into the flesh of the mangos helps quench a little of our thirst, but it's not enough—nowhere near it. Two days ago, we were in heaven, today, not so much. We haven't made it over the pass, we've finished off the last of the fruit, and desperately need to figure something out. If the others really are scoping us out like Graham suspects, they're probably laughing at our failure.

"We have to get water today," Graham says.

"Yes." I try to say as few words as possible now, because of the dryness of my mouth and throat.

It hurts to even try speaking. "Dizzy," I say, holding a hand to my head.

"Me too."

We meet each other's eyes. There's nothing stopping us from going back to the others. We're not *banished*. We left on our own—supposed to be getting around the damn cliff, and no one said we couldn't come back. *Maybe we should...*

Graham shakes his head as if reading my thoughts. "Tom," he says.

I nod. *Tom.*

WE WAIT until night to move, the cool air a comfort to our overheated skin. The moon and stars light our way back down the beach to the others—our only choice if we want water.

After hours of walking, the dehydration starts to get to me. I stop with one hand out to balance myself against the dizziness and one hand against my head. "Are you okay?" Graham asks.

"I just need a minute." I wait for the world to stop spinning then we continue.

It seems nothing's changed with the others. Everything looks the same. They still have the same shelter—although it looks like it's been repaired since the storm, and just like us, still no fire.

"You take left, I'll take right," Graham whispers.

We spread out, expecting the water to be hidden like before, but it doesn't take long for us to find it. A backpack filled to the brim is sitting just outside the shelter along with the bottles.

When I see it just sitting there out in the open, so beautiful and tasty, waiting to be devoured, I can't help but lick my lips. I motion for Graham. He notices my wave and responds with one of his own, holding up a water bottle.

I suck in a breath, grab the backpack, and meet him across the camp where the others won't hear us. Before either of us speaks, we split an entire water bottle. We're both panting, water dribbling down our chins. It's the best water we've ever tasted.

"Any sign of the other backpack?" I whisper.

Graham frowns and shakes his head. "No. I haven't seen our bags either."

I purse my lips. "Do you think they're hiding them?"

"They must be. I don't understand why they would, though, and not hide their water too."

"What about any of the bananas? Have you seen those? I didn't."

He shakes his head again. "No. They're either out and getting really hungry or hiding them with our stuff."

I sigh. "What do we do now, then?"

"We take what's owed to us. They took our supplies, so we take theirs."

I start to shake my head. I can't do that to them, no matter what they've done to us, to Tom. "How can we live with ourselves if we take the rest of what they have? We're all on this island together. I can't do it, Graham."

"They did it to us!"

"It doesn't matter. I just can't."

His lips thin in anger. "Fine. We need to take *something*, though. At least just to carry water for ourselves."

"Okay. A few of the water bottles then."

He huffs, annoyed, but nods. We're in agreement.

I return the backpack to its spot by the shelter while Graham tries to hide our tracks. If they know we were here, they'll come for retaliation—or so we believe. Each carrying two water bottles, we head into the forest toward the stream.

CHAPTER TWENTY-THREE

THE FOREST IS SO MUCH different from the beach at night. I knew going in that it would be creepy, but I had no idea just *how much.*

On the beach, the moon lit our path. Here in the forest, the canopy of the trees blocks out most of the light. Critters scurry in the dark under our feet, and I'm glad I can't see them.

All I can think about is *what is living out here?* I'm terrified of stepping on a snake or something deadly enough to kill me or eat me. The feeling of being watched grips me, just like before. This is why we haven't camped here at night. I grasp onto Graham like he's a lifeline, although I'm sure he's just as nervous as me.

"We have to be careful by the water," he says. "Animals will want to drink from it too, so we need to watch our backs."

"What kind of—" I gulp. "Predator do you think lives here?"

"I'm not sure. I've never been stuck on an island in the Bahamas to find out."

I frown at his stupid joke. "This is serious."

"Sorry, trying to lighten the mood. Seriously though, I don't know."

"Do you think we can catch something? We can't survive off of fruit. We need substance."

"I don't know how to trap. Do you?"

I sigh. "No."

"Don't worry. We'll look to see if any bananas have fallen, and who knows, maybe we'll get lucky and snatch a crab like we talked about."

"Are you—Graham, I'm not sure I can go to the bananas."

He's silent for a few seconds and then says, "I know. But it's for our survival. You can wait on the path, and I'll look by the tree. There's probably nothing, anyway."

We continue. Glowing eyes watch us but to our immense relief, nothing tries to attack. We reach the banana tree, where I stay back and let Graham check for fallen fruit. I feel like a coward, but I can't bring myself to go over there.

"Anything?" I ask when Graham returns.

"There's a couple, but they're picked over and rotted."

"Okay. Let's go." I didn't really expect there to be anything edible for us, but it's still a disappointment. I don't like being in this spot—this place has a bad vibe to it. I can't stop seeing Tom sprawled there at an awkward angle—lifeless. It kills me what happened to him and more, *why*.

I pull Graham away, and we continue the rest of the way to the stream. When we reach it, we drink our fill again. I have second thoughts about what we've been doing and how long it's been taking us to do it.

"It feels like we're not even trying," I say.

"What do you mean? Of course we're trying. What else are we doing here?" Graham seems annoyed at my words, but I'm annoyed too. I'm annoyed that we're still here, still doing this, still worrying about water, when we should be far across to the other side of the island by now.

"We've been at it for days and have gotten nowhere. What have we even been doing? I think we need to say to hell with the dangers at night and start camping in the forest. I think it's the only way we're going to be able to move forward."

"To hell with the dangers? We don't have any idea what's out here. We still don't have a fire going. What are we supposed to do when a predator decides we look like a tasty meal?"

"Honestly, Graham, at this point, I don't care. I'd rather be a tasty meal than be trapped here forever because I can't even make it all the way around to make sure there's no other way." I put my hands on his shoulders to pull him closer. "We're out here now, aren't we?"

He finally nods with the realization that what I'm saying is true. "Yeah. You're right." He hugs me and says, "Tomorrow. We'll plan on doing this right."

I'm filled with relief. It feels like an enormous weight has been lifted from my shoulders and I can finally breathe a little easier. It's not just that he's agreed with my idea—it's that he listened to what I was saying. He was willing to admit that I was right and change the plan accordingly.

You're a good person, Graham. I don't have the courage to say it out loud, but I hope the smile I give him shows him what I'm thinking.

We allow ourselves to rest after gathering the water, but we know we can't stay too long. The others will be waking with the sunrise, and we don't want to be anywhere around when they find they've had visitors in the night.

PART 2

MARCELLA

CHAPTER TWENTY-FOUR

THE SOUND of heated whispers wakes me. I want to groan my frustration but I'm too thirsty. Any sound I make is a drain on my already dry throat, so I stay silent, complaining internally instead. *Why does there always have to be something going wrong?*

Wade and Caleb are a few feet away, arguing. "What are we supposed to do?" Caleb hisses.

Wade says something too low for me to make out.

"We need to go after them!"

"Stay—" *Goddammit, Wade, talk louder!*

"Don't fucking tell me to calm down!"

I flinch at Caleb's tone. This entire time he's maintained a calm demeanor, even after what happened to Tom. He's been cool—in control, even taking charge at times. *This* is nothing like him. I glance at Lauren, still sleeping and I wonder if she knows there seems to be another side to the person she's so close to. A side that's fully capable of panic, *and who knows what else,* just like the rest of us.

I'm torn between wanting to overhear more of Wade and Caleb's conversation, wanting to go back to sleep, and wanting to yell at them to shut the hell up. One of them is coming this way. Without thinking, I lie back down and pretend to be asleep.

"Hey, wake up!" Caleb calls.

I wait for Lauren to move first but she's still snoring softly, so I stay put too.

"Wake up!" he yells again, louder this time.

Lauren stretches. "What's wrong?" she asks, groggy, barely awake.

"We have a situation out here. We need to talk."

Anger rises in my chest like molten lava when he kicks my foot. I'm on the verge of putting him in his place but hold my tongue. Instead, I follow Lauren's suit, stretching and giving a fake yawn. "Give me a minute to wake up," I groan.

"Hurry the hell up. This is important." He turns on his heel and leaves.

"Who died and made him king?" I say under my breath. I know I'm no comedian, but I think that comment earns me at least a snicker or puff of air, maybe at least a nod of agreement. His total three-sixty mood shift doesn't sit well with me.

Instead, Lauren gives a choked sob.

I turn to her, alarmed. "What's wrong?"

She shakes her head with a hand to her throat.

"Lauren?"

"Nothing. I'm fine." She grimaces. "We better see what's going on."

We get up to meet the guys. Wade is lying on the sand beneath a palm tree, his hands tucked under the back of his head. He looks relaxed, like he's on vacation and doesn't have a care in the world.

Caleb looks the total opposite. He's pacing in front of Wade, fidgeting, scratching at his hair, mumbling something to himself. He looks agitated and I wonder what would put him this out of sorts. Our entire situation is a living nightmare, but it took *this*, whatever this is, to finally push him over the edge.

Lauren reaches out a hand to him, but he bats her away.

"Hey, don't be an asshole," I say. I turn to Lauren. "Let's go for a walk until he can change his attitude."

"Hang on a minute," Wade says. He gives Caleb a look. "Caleb is out of line but he's right. We need to talk."

"What's going on?" Lauren asks, looking pale.

Wade sits up and sighs. "It seems one of us got thirsty in the middle of the night."

"I told you, it wasn't—" Caleb starts.

Wade continues. "Did either of you take a drink last night?"

Lauren and I look at each other then shake our heads. "Are you accusing us of something?" I ask.

"The water is gone," Caleb says, throwing his hands in the air, staring at us with bulging eyes.

"What do you mean *gone?*"

"Fucking gone. G-o-n-e. Bye-bye. Adios!" He waves his hands around to show he's holding on to nothing.

"We can just get more, can't we?" Lauren says.

"Sadly, no," Wade says. "All the water bottles are gone."

My eyes go wide. There seems to be only one explanation, but I can't believe it. *They wouldn't do that to us.* "All of them? Are you sure?"

Wade grimaces. "Yeah. We're sure."

"What now?" Lauren asks, almost whispering.

"We have two choices," he says. "One, we move our camp to the stream until we can figure out another solution."

"But the ship—"

He holds up a hand. "Yeah. It would mean possibly missing the ship if it comes back."

I scowl at the word *if*. "The second choice?" I ask.

"Payback," Caleb says.

We all look at each other, all understanding the thing that hasn't been said, the accusation that hasn't been spoken. *Erin and Graham did this.*

"We can't know that this was them," I say. "We're assuming."

Caleb gives a cruel laugh. "I'm sorry, do you see anyone else here? Do you think maybe poor Tom got thirsty in the middle of the night? Why else would they slink off in the dark without saying goodbye?"

Lauren gasps. "Caleb!"

"Maybe it was you," I say. "Maybe you did this and you're trying to blame them."

He stares at me, not bothering to deny it.

I look at Wade, who's watching Caleb. "What do you think we should do?" I ask him.

He turns to me. "I think we should move to the stream. Even if it was them, for whatever reason, we still need water. We can get a refill of bananas while we're at it."

"How? Our only tree climber is over there in the sand— dead. Or did you forget about that? And what happens then?" Caleb continues. "We stay at the stream forever? Camp out until we die of malnutrition or until we're so old we can't move anymore? We miss any chance of rescue if we do that. We're basically signing our lives away."

"I don't think we are," Lauren says, finding her voice. "If they do come for us, they'll probably circle the island. We'll hear them, I'm sure of it. And we can leave an SOS in the sand."

"That's a good idea," I say. "We can make it huge, so a helicopter can see it."

The three of us are in agreement. It doesn't matter right

now if it was Graham and Erin, or what their motives were. Even if it was one of us, for whatever psychotic reason, it doesn't matter right now. The only thing that *does* matter is not dying of dehydration. We have to get to the stream.

Caleb doesn't seem to be getting it through his head though. "I can't believe this," he says. "You're just going to let them do this to us and get away with it? They as good as left us for dead!"

"How's that?" Wade asks. "If it was them, they knew we knew about the stream."

Caleb clenches his fists, opens his mouth to speak, but Lauren rushes to say, "Maybe there's a reason." She takes a step toward Caleb. "Maybe they found water, and it's better. Maybe we should go to them not for revenge, but for help."

"She has a good point," I say. "Maybe there's something to it that we're not thinking of."

"Or they took *ours* because they *don't* have any." Caleb looks at us like we both have screws loose. "Look, all this talking is making me thirsty. Let's get the water, then we'll figure out whatever comes next."

Finally, we all agree.

CHAPTER TWENTY-FIVE

Bugs are the story of my life now. I see them every waking hour, hear and feel them when I'm asleep, and I'm sure I've eaten a few by mistake. They're *everywhere*. I'm so consumed by them, I'm starting to imagine writing them into my next novel. *Maybe my heroine will build a flamethrower and torch them all.*

"It's been two days," Caleb says. "We need to make a move. Now."

I swat a mosquito off my arm and scratch at the bites on my leg.

"What move?" Lauren says.

"We know they have the bottles. We need to go get them back."

"We don't know anything," Wade says.

"No, *you* don't know anything," Caleb growls.

"Wade's right, we don't know for sure. But Caleb's right too. We can't stay here. I'd rather die of thirst than get eaten alive by these fucking bugs." I say. I hold back a scream as something with too many legs crawls across my foot.

"Can we forget the water for two seconds and talk about

how the hell we're getting out of here?" Lauren says. "We need to stop trying to make ourselves comfortable and *do* something to get out of here. Andrew isn't coming back for us."

"That's exactly what Erin was trying to say before we all shot her down," Wade says.

We're all silent, considering our options.

"Graham has the flare gun," Caleb says.

Wade plays with his beard as he thinks. "We said it was best to wait on using that."

"If we're building a raft, we're going to need it."

"We can build a raft here, where we'll have plenty of supplies—" Lauren starts.

Caleb barks a laugh.

"We'll have all the water we need and food, too. And then we can carry it in sections to the beach once we're ready," she continues.

"And food? What food? You mean bugs and rotten bananas?"

"And the flare gun?" I ask, ignoring Caleb.

"We can split up. Two of us build, two go get the gun?" Lauren says.

"Or we can stick together. Get the gun once the raft is done?" Wade says. "The raft is going to be a lot of work and the longer we take to build it, the farther away our ship gets."

"And the closer another storm gets," I say.

At that, we all look up to see the gray clouds overhead. *It's storm season, alright.* The last storm didn't go so well, and we all know it.

"So, do we agree then? Raft first?" Wade says after a pause.

Caleb nods grudgingly.

Lauren nods.

"Yeah," I say.

"Alright then, any ideas on a design?"

Caleb goes to his backpack and pulls out a pad of paper and pen. "What kind of writer would I be if I didn't have a good ole fashioned pen and paper?"

I redden at the offhanded insult. "Not everyone is old school, Caleb."

He only laughs and starts drawing. We wait to see what he comes up with before we each give our own suggestions on how it might be improved. By the time we're done, we have an outline for a raft made of the largest branches we can find, room for all of us—Erin and Graham too, if we all sit with our legs in the water.

It's dangerous, but also the only way we figure we'll get it big enough without falling apart. Our design requires us to use palm leaves and strips of the strongest vines we can find to bind it together. If we have to, we can use strips of clothing or our backpacks, but we're hoping it doesn't come to that because we're relying on them for food storage.

"Alright, folks, let's get to it," Caleb says, clapping his hands.

"We should pair up to grab some of the bigger branches. Why don't you and Lauren team up that way and Wade and I can check over here," I say, pointing to an area of the forest.

Lauren gives me a brief shake of her head, but Caleb says, "Good idea."

"Lauren can start collecting our binding materials, too," Wade says, noticing her nod too.

"OK, I'll—" she starts.

"How am I going to carry anything then?" Caleb says. "No, she'll come with me."

"You can come with us. We can get some massive ones with the three of us," Wade says.

Caleb looks between the three of us, pausing. "We should pair up like you said. Let's see what we can get to start with."

I meet Lauren's gaze. She looks worried. *Why?*

Caleb has been acting off for days now. Something is going on with him and she knows what's up. If she's afraid to be alone with him, maybe there's a good reason.

I start to offer to go with them, I'm sure Wade won't mind, but Lauren nods to me, accepting the situation. Whatever's going on between the two of them, she'll have to handle it on her own.

CHAPTER TWENTY-SIX

THERE's something in the forest—something watching us. I know how it sounds, but I'm not going crazy. I know it's there and *it* might not be an it.

We have most of the big logs that we need for the raft, now we're working on binding. We've decided to separate in order to cover more ground. *Why did we do that again?* I'm starting to wonder at our logic.

Something rustles next to me. "Hello?" I call. *It could be one of the others.* No. I don't think so. Whatever—whoever this is, it's trying to stay hidden. It's not here to collect palm leaves or anything else.

I give a nonchalant shrug and move on. *If it's watching me, I don't want it to know I'm onto it.* Gradually, I work my way toward one of the others. Wade is supposed to be nearest.

A branch breaks. My hands start to sweat. "Hey, Wade?" I call.

"Yeah?" His voice is faint but hearing him bolsters my courage.

Two possibilities run through my mind. One, that this is a predator, here to hunt its dinner. And two, that it's Erin and, or Graham. If it is them, who knows what the hell they want but I'm not trying to find out while I'm alone. Isolation can do things to people. If they're capable of taking all our water, who knows what else they're capable of.

"Wade, I'm coming to you."

"Okay," he calls back, a little less faint.

Good. I'm moving in the right direction. I keep going, stopping every now and then to casually collect something that looks useful. My arms are full, but the weight is relatively light.

Something is following me. Footsteps aren't far behind. My head turns automatically, a gut reaction, and that's when I run into the low-hanging limb. Whatever or whoever it is has to know I'm onto it now.

I stumble, dizzy from the impact. Blood from my nose is leaking down my face but I'm more worried about not falling and dropping everything to wipe it away.

I listen, my eyes shifting, scanning the trees. There's nothing. No sound, as if everything out here is holding its breath.

Time to go, Marcella. I force myself to keep going, faster this time, paying more attention so I don't run into a goddamn tree again. "Wade?" I call his name again, expecting him to be close.

For a moment, he doesn't answer. Panic starts to rise in me, intensifying with each second that passes. I wait, then call again. "Where are you?"

Again, I listen, straining to take in any sound. I hold my breath, trying to ignore the pounding of my own heart. *Please be okay, please be okay!*

"I'm here!" he finally answers. Not as close as I'd hoped, but close.

I release my breath and bridge the gap between us. When I reach him, I whisper, "I think there's something out here."

He raises an eyebrow at me. "It's a forest... of course there is."

"No, I mean like a bear or—"

Wade laughs. "There are no bears on this island, Marcella."

I grab his arm, lean forward, and whisper, "Listen to me. Something or *someone* was watching me." I give him a look, hoping he understands my meaning.

He yanks his arm from me, taking a step back with a look of disgust. "How many times do I have to tell you to keep your fucking hands to yourself? Cut that shit out before someone sees." He gives me a look so filled with rage that I take a step back.

"Don't worry, Erin isn't here to see."

He walks away, leaving me alone again.

I clench my fists at my side, digging my fingernails in hard enough for me to focus on the pain radiating through my hands. The wind is starting to pick up. I close my eyes, listening but no longer able to tell if someone is out there watching.

"Erin, if that's you, I'm sorry," I say.

Silence.

"I'm sorry for everything. I should've been a better friend when I had the chance."

My nails dig harder. Warm blood leaks out onto my fingers, but I don't let up.

CHAPTER TWENTY-SEVEN

Rain falls in torrents as we carry completed sections of the raft back to the beach. Carrying them over our heads to shield us from most of the rain, we slowly make our way through the forest, back to the beach. The entire time, I constantly look over my shoulder, trying to peer into the trees.

Not knowing is plaguing me. *What's out there? Who's out there? Is there anyone at all or am I starting to lose it?* None of the others have mentioned anything. I wonder if they're doing the same as me—denying what they hear, what they feel, afraid to be judged by the rest of us.

With the rain and everything else, it's too loud to hear, but I still feel those eyes. *Something hungry.* I pick up my pace when the gap between the others grows too big for comfort.

What if it's not Erin? What if I'm right about it really being a creature of some kind, prowling the forest, waiting for us to make the wrong move? Either I'm the only one who notices it, or someone else does too—either way, no one has said a word about it.

"What do you keep looking at?" Lauren asks, making me jump.

I have to yell to be heard over the rain. "Nothing." I shake my head. "I mean, I don't see anything, but I'm not sure what it is I'm looking for."

She raises her eyebrows in interest. "Care to explain?"

Better to spit it out than say nothing and watch everyone get eaten. "I heard something a few days ago and... I've felt it watching me—watching probably all of us." My face reddens at how the statement sounds. I'm not sure how I would react if someone said the same thing to me—probably with a bitchy, smart-assed remark. I wouldn't blame her if she did the same.

Lauren's face drains of color. Instead of laughing me off, she takes me seriously.

I rush to add, "I didn't want anyone to panic. I didn't see anything, so I mean, I could just be—"

"No. I believe you," she says.

I let out a breath. "I said something to Wade, but he didn't want to listen. I figured it was best to wait until I actually saw something."

Lauren clenches her jaw. She pauses before saying, "Wade isn't the boss of us. That might sound childish but just because he doesn't want to listen doesn't mean there's not something else going on. Next time, don't let him bully you into silence."

"Oh, no, it wasn't like that—"

"Come on, we better catch up," she says, looking around.

The gap between the others has widened again, now to the point that they're out of sight. Lauren and I each adjust the makeshift section of raft over our heads while attempting to pick up the pace.

The wood chafes my hands. Splinters are lodged beneath my skin. I try to ignore them, but my fingers keep slipping and every time I readjust it gets worse.

There's a crash up ahead of us. Still out of sight, the guys are yelling at each other, cussing. Caleb's voice rises above everything else. "—kill you, asshole!"

Lauren turns to me with huge, panicked eyes. "We have to go!" she cries, dropping her portion of the raft. It hits the ground, ripping my section out of my hands without warning.

I scream as the bark skins the palms of my hands. The part of the raft we were carrying moments ago, hits the ground. The binding rips apart, setting the logs free to scatter across the forest floor.

I'm torn between a desperate need to stop everything from falling apart and helping Lauren to prevent Caleb and Wade from murdering each other. As I watch her run away, leaving me alone, *again,* the latter urge wins.

"Wait!" I yell after her, trying to avoid looking at our failure.

"He's going to do something stupid!" she calls back over her shoulder.

Her fear is so real, I wonder again what she knows about Caleb that the rest of us don't. He's been out of it lately, but we all have, and with good reason. *Especially after what happened to Tom. I never should've left her alone with him that day.*

Lauren and I climb a hill, the men's voices grow louder as we approach. "Caleb!" Lauren calls.

They lower their voices to heated whispers, words no longer intelligible.

"Lauren, wait!" I try to stop her, but I'm too slow.

At the base of the hill, Wade and Caleb stand with a third man, his back to us. Lauren and I both stop short. "Graham?" she says. "Where's Erin?"

The man turns to look at us. My jaw drops. The man isn't

Graham. It's Andrew—Lauren's friend, the one who brought us here.

"I'd like to know the same thing," he says before pointing a gun at Lauren and pulling the trigger.

PART 3

ANDREW

Sixteen days ago

CHAPTER TWENTY-EIGHT

I ʜᴜᴍ to myself as the seven individuals disembark the tender. *This is going to be so good.* I try to keep the grin from showing on my face—wouldn't want to give anything away. I play it as casual as possible, letting my false concern shine through, along with a little confidence. They always like to see that.

The money the group scrounged together to *get me to do this* is pitiful. It's chump change compared to what I'm really getting paid. But hey, a little bonus cash never hurt anyone. *It's not like they're going to be needing it.*

"Have a productive day, guys. I'll see you tonight!" I call when the last of them is gone. I smile and wave, watching how each of them has their own secret reservations but none willing to call it off.

"Remember, only shoot the flare if someone is dead!" Russ calls next to me.

I give him a look, trying not to laugh.

He shrugs, full of innocence. "What?"

How long will it take them to break? I wonder. *Probably not long. It's never very long.*

"Let's get out of here, Russ."

We pull away from the small, broken dock at full speed, headed back for the cruise ship. I continue to hum to myself, counting all the dollar bills coming my way. This time has been easy—one of the easiest yet, but it's nowhere near over. This is just the start.

"Cut that shit out," Russ says.

"What? You don't like my singing voice?"

"No, I don't."

"You're always so worried. The money is already ours. What's eating you?"

"You're not worried at all?"

"Nope." I brush the imaginary lint off my shoulder. "It's a done deal."

The lifeboat bounces as we hit wave after wave on our way back to the ship. Russ and I both hang on but it's nothing we're not used to. We travel the rest of the distance in silence, I'm thinking about the profits, and I'm sure Russ is thinking about the consequences of getting caught.

When we reach the ship, I bring out my satellite phone to text.

It's done. We're back.

Moments later, I get a notification that a deposit has been made into my checking account. I grin as I say to Russ, "It's payday, my friend." We shake hands and part ways.

IN THE CAPTAIN'S private quarters, I wait. A message was sent to him a few minutes ago, *requesting* a private audience. And by requesting, I mean demanding.

There are no choices here. Only orders. No *yes* or *no*, only *when*.

The steady rhythm of ticks coming from the clock on the wall is grating on my nerves. I check the time—he's five minutes late. I hope he's not going to be a problem.

Finally, the cabin door swings open. "Sorry, sorry, I know you don't like to wait," the captain says.

"It's not me, Cap, you know that."

"Right, of course." He shuffles around the room, fixing himself a drink from the minibar, adjusting his uniform. "Drink?" he asks, already knowing I'll decline.

"No. Now, if you don't mind, we have matters to discuss."

His eyes flash. It's clear he doesn't care for me, but frankly, I don't care if he does or not. It's not his job to like me, it's his job to take the orders given and complete them. He has a singular purpose here and he *can* be replaced if necessary.

"The ship is already on course. We set sail the moment the call came through."

"Good. And the tracking?"

"Taken care of. If anyone looks, they think we're in the middle of the Atlantic."

"Excellent." I award him with a winning smile. "Everything else is going according to plan, I take it?"

He gives a firm nod. "Yes. Everything is right on track. The rest of the passengers are none the wiser."

"And you understand what you are to do if there's a problem?"

"Kill anyone who gets in the way."

"That's right."

"I get the picture, Andrew." He glowers at me, and I'm not

sure I quite like his tone. He's almost challenging me. I can tell he's got a little sass in him, but so far, he's done as he's been told. It's not my job to hire these people, but it is my job to make sure they follow through.

I give him a warning look while I watch him take a sip from his drink. "You should receive your payment within the next hour. Your job is considered complete as soon as we reach our next port."

"Wonderful," he says. "Anything else I need to know about?"

"If there is, I'll tell you when you need to know."

His mouth falls. "How about you tell me who else on my ship is a part of this?"

"Now what makes you think there is anyone else?"

He scoffs. "Come on. There's no way you and I are the only ones."

"It doesn't matter one way or another. You don't need to know." I smile and lean back against the wall with my arms crossed.

"It would be nice to know if someone is just doing their part or is up to something else. This is still my ship and security is real despite this little side mission."

I take a second to pretend to think about his concerns. I stroke my chin and twist my lips from side to side as if it's a hard decision to make. The captain's eyes light up slightly, as if he really believes I might tell him what he wants to know.

The real question here is *why does he want to know?* His part is done. Why does he care at this point? *Security* is a bullshit answer. I don't buy it.

I let out a sigh and start to shake my head. "It's a shame, Cap."

"What—" He starts to cough. He keeps coughing and his

eyes bulge when he realizes he can't stop. The more he goes on, the worse it gets until blood starts to spray from his mouth.

"I was hoping the poison wouldn't be necessary. I hate being right but alas, I usually am. That's why they pay me the big bucks, Cap."

He reaches for me. I sidestep with little effort. He falls to the floor, now silent, no longer coughing—no longer breathing.

I bring out my phone to send a text.

Captain taken care of.

I send a second message to a different number.

Ready for you.

Russ enters the room with a cleaning cart. "Long time no see," he says.

"I tried to keep it clean for you."

He gets to work while I leave the room.

CHAPTER TWENTY-NINE

THERE'S a new captain aboard now, no hiccups so far. Today, the entire ship is scheduled to disembark, back to our regularly planned itinerary. I double-check the message on my phone, giving me instructions on where to go once on land.

Russ gives me a nod as I walk out onto the dock. He stays with the ship to ensure that that end is tied firmly into its knot. For the next part, I'm on my own.

NASSAU IS COVERED IN TOURISTS, despite the time of year. People don't care if it's *storm* season. They care if they can get a good deal on a vacation. I smile to myself, remembering how easy it was to *hook Lauren and her colleagues up with those cheap tickets.*

I wipe the sweat from my forehead as I sit in the back of a taxi, bringing out my phone to text.

On my way.

"You come from one of those ships?" the driver asks, making casual conversation.

"No. I'm a photographer. I just take pictures of them." I hold up the Canon camera hanging from my neck.

He glances at me in the rearview mirror. "You American?"

"Canadian."

"Ah."

We ride the rest of the way in silence until my stop comes and I leave him with a generous tip. Not too much so I'll stand out, but enough so he might keep his mouth shut if anyone came asking any questions.

They won't. But it doesn't hurt to have extra coverage on the rear end. And besides, I'm feeling generous today.

There's almost nothing around but resorts. Hotel after hotel rises into the sky, as far down the road as the eye can see. Now that I'm out of the air-conditioned car, I'm covered in sweat again. I pull out my handkerchief to dab my forehead. It's going to be a few blocks I have to walk in this heat. The humidity doesn't agree with me, but I'm getting paid too much to complain.

When I'm finally at the building, I send a text.

Here.

It's one of the many resorts on the island and the meeting place might be anywhere inside. I take a seat at one of the bars and order myself a whiskey neat while I wait. I sip from my glass while the cameras above monitor my every move.

They're making sure I wasn't followed. Not only that, but

that everything that needs to be in line is. Once they're able to verify, I'll be able to move forward.

It might take hours, might take all day, or it might take a few minutes. There's no way for me to know, so I make myself comfortable, moving from the bar into a cushioned seat by a window. I keep a close eye on everyone who passes, wondering if they're watching me too.

Eventually, a message comes through.

Penthouse.

I get up and head for the elevator.

"ANDREW, WELCOME," a woman says as I enter the room. I've seen her before—she was a maid on the ship.

She leads me to where a group of investors are meeting. I have no idea who they are, if this is all of them or only a small portion. I'll probably never know and don't really have a desire to, either. It's just the way things are done.

"Well done so far, Andrew," one of them says. He's dressed in a button-down tropical shirt, sunglasses hanging out the front.

I smile at the praise, bowing my head slightly. "Thank you, sir."

"Good eye on the captain too," another says—this one in a pink tank top, his beer belly on the verge of hanging out.

"Just doing my job, sir," I say with false modesty. I know damn well if I let something like that slip, I'd be the one getting cleaned up off the floor.

"Keep it up, and there might be a bonus for you at the end," a third says, this one fit like a bodybuilder, good-looking too. Unlike the others, all dressed like tourists on vacation, he's dressed in a suit. I notice for the first time that he's the only one dressed so formally, and I admonish myself for not seeing it before. This one—this is his baby this time. They always take it more seriously when it's their baby.

I give them what they want, a show of being impressed, being flattered, honored to have such high praise from them. They throw money around like it doesn't matter. Because it doesn't—not to them.

"Thank you so much, sir!" I say. "You know you can rely on me to see this through." Of course they know it. If they didn't, I wouldn't be here. But that's beside the point. These guys like to have their asses kissed and with the amount of money they're throwing my way, that's something I don't mind doing. Not at all.

"Have a seat, Andrew. Make yourself at home," tropical shirt man says.

Pink tank top guy grins. "This is the best part."

I move to take a seat in one of the plush leather chairs. We're all facing the same direction—toward an entire length of a wall covered in nothing but monitors. One large one in the middle, surrounded by many smaller ones.

"Is this where they set up camp?" I ask.

"It's every inch of their entire island," suit man says.

I eye one of the smaller screens at the bottom. At first glance, it looks like a picture of the forest, but just as I start to look away, there's movement. I focus, waiting for it to come again. Then, a dark figure, completely camouflaged, moves across the screen.

Pink tank top man notices me staring. "We have people in place to make things a little more interesting."

"Oh?"

"They instill a little fear—stalk them, chase them, steal supplies, make them turn on each other. Stuff like that."

"Hardly necessary," tropical shirt man adds. "Since the lost do most of the work themselves, but the viewers love it."

CHAPTER THIRTY

As LONG AS they're on that island, I'm going to be here in this penthouse. I don't mind, really. It's comfortable, plenty of food, and most importantly—air-conditioned. Dealing with the investors and playing the part of the simpering nobody employee is tiring, but I only have to do it for a little while longer.

Things are wrapping up nicely. One of them is dead, two of them are having sex, and resources are limited. They're starting to turn on each other as expected.

"Andrew," pink shirt man calls. "You didn't tell all of them, did you? I'm going to lose a ton of money if you did."

I shake my head. "No, sir. I made sure to be careful. I only told who I was instructed to tell."

"Good, good. You followed the rest of the list as instructed?"

"Yes, sir." *Of course I did. I'm not new at this.* They tell me exactly who to tell and who not to, *what* to tell and what *not* to, so the question surprises me.

"How do you get them to go along with it every time?" tropical shirt man asks.

"I make sure they know there's a ton of money in it for them, of course, sir."

They all laugh at that.

"I love to see their faces when the ship is gone. They never realize that part's coming. It gets me every time!" pink shirt man says.

"I like to keep it a surprise, sir," I say, grinning.

"Keep it up, Andrew."

I wonder which of the group the investors are most interested in. I know they can request people to be included in the game, and I have my suspicions, but I never know for sure who the main person of interest is or if there even is one. Sometimes there is, sometimes there isn't.

DAYS PASS AS we watch the activities on the island. Each of the investors spends time on a laptop or on a cell phone, constantly in contact with others. This is entertainment to them, but also business. I hate to think how much money they make.

Eventually, the time comes where things are slowing down too much—not enough death or sex, or action. Even the camouflaged people in the forest have exhausted their role.

"You're going to have to go down there and get things moving," pink tank top man says, and suddenly it's clear as day why they've kept me here this whole time, my purpose for staying so long.

"Won't that interfere with the game, sir? I thought—"

"*We* make the game," he growls, angry with my nerve to

question an order. "If we say to do it, then that's what we want."

"Don't worry, Andrew," tropical shirt man says. "It will only add another dimension. Surprises like this are ideal. Things are too slow right now and that's not good for anyone." He gives me a pointed look.

I look between them, solidly put in my place. I don't want to do this. It puts me in a bad position. But I also don't have a choice and I know better than to ask questions. There's almost nothing they hate more than being questioned.

If I say that I won't go, I might wind up there with them anyway. Either that, or they'll just outright shoot me. It's better to submit—*always*.

"Okay, sir. I'll do it."

"Good man."

"Andrew," suit man says. "Tell them that they can share Tom's money between them. Make it clear that since he died the money is available to split."

The investors all gape at him. They share sly looks with each other. "By God, I swear you're a genius," tropical shirt man says.

Suit man gives a shrug. "Just adding a little more spice to the pot."

"They're going to tear each other apart."

"That's the point, isn't it?" pink tank top man says. "Anyone up for some bets?"

"You're okay with them knowing who else knows?" I ask.

"If you can keep the ruse, keep it. Pick who you tell in private, see what happens."

"Yes, sir."

While they discuss the matter among themselves, I rise from my seat, take one last look at the wall of monitors to note everyone's whereabouts, then move to leave.

"Thanks again, Andrew," tropical shirt man says before I'm gone. The way he always seems to take charge makes me wonder if this is his baby after all.

"Shall I come back when I'm done?" I ask.

"Why don't you stay there to see this through."

I nod to him then leave the room, my fate sealed. Either I do my job well, or I won't be leaving that island at all—I may become one of the lost. *I won't let that happen.* I'm going to give these fucking investors everything they want, and more. They want action? I'll make sure they get it in spades.

PART 4

GRAHAM

CHAPTER THIRTY-ONE

A GUNSHOT RINGS out across the island, making my blood run cold. Erin and I stop midstep, halfway down a steep incline. She looks at me with eyes full of fear. "Graham... was that what I think it was?"

I try to unclench my jaw, but it seems stuck and all I can do is nod.

"Oh my god! How'd they get a gun on the ship? Who do you think shot it? *Why* would they be shooting?" She throws her hands in the air, realizing how useful it could've been from the beginning. "Why the hell didn't they use it to hunt for some food? Forget the goddamn *bananas!* Or we could've gotten the ship's attention!" She huffs, out of breath but bursting at the seams with more unanswered questions.

I clear my throat, trying to think of something useful to say. "I don't know. I'm sure as hell glad to be over here though."

"You don't think—" Erin grimaces, drawing a finger across her throat in a *killing* gesture.

"Maybe not. But I can't see any other reason for it to be kept a secret."

She gasps, grabs hold of my arm. "You don't think this is our fault, do you? What if we started this because of the water?"

"No, it has to be something else. If that was the case, they could've killed us when they stole all our supplies."

"But we don't know they took—"

"They did."

Erin presses her lips together. It's obvious she still doesn't agree, but I'm also glad she's not going to stand here and argue about it all day when it doesn't matter anymore. "Let's go," she says, continuing down the hill.

It's been a struggle, a battle for days, but we're finally going to make it to the other side. She was right about spending the night in the forest. It's been the only way for us to get this far and without her pushing the issue, I think we would've been stuck there on that beach a lot longer if we wouldn't have finally taken the risk.

I don't mind letting Erin lead the way. She's good at it and I like the view. Win, win if you ask me.

We keep going until the terrain finally levels back out before stopping to drink. "I'm so glad we went back for more," Erin says between gulps. "I hope you're right. I hope whatever we heard back there had nothing to do with us. If it did, I don't think we're going to be safe over here for very long."

"I'm glad too. We never would've made it without another fill-up. And I don't want you to think about *what-ifs*. We need to focus on the task and if one of them shows up with a gun, we'll take care of them together."

"I still feel bad about taking the bottles from them." She wipes droplets from her mouth then twists the cap back on her bottle. She meets my gaze. "I trust you, Graham."

"You'd feel worse if you didn't have water in your belly," I say dryly, trying not to choke.

Erin smiles. "You know, I'm starting to really like you, Graham."

I try to keep my face from showing my emotions. I struggle against the automatic reaction of my muscles, turning away from her so she can't see. "Likewise," I manage to say.

"My marriage was—complicated. Let's just say it's been an adjustment, and I want you to know I don't expect anything from you. I like you and that's that, okay?"

"Oh, I got it," I say, swatting at her ass. "Now, get trekkin'. The beach is calling our names."

She laughs and continues on.

I start to notice the way some of the trees are farther apart. It seems there's a clearing of some kind ahead. Erin notices too. She picks up her pace to a jog.

"It might be nothing," I pant after her, trying to keep up.

"It's water!" she screams at the top of her lungs.

I wince but can't help grinning. Neither of us misses the sound of the waterfall.

ERIN'S RIGHT. There is water. There's a waterfall spilling into a *lake*, with so much water we could live here if we wanted. We can swim and bathe and drink until we explode. My eyes are tearing up at the sight of it, my mouth salivating.

Erin breaks out into laughter. She throws her arms around my neck, kisses me all over—my cheeks, forehead, mouth. My chest clenches.

I hold her to me, then toss her into the lake, laughing with her as I follow her in.

CHAPTER THIRTY-TWO

"ARE you really writing a book about an evil cat?" Erin asks, pushing the hair from her face.

I adjust the arm she's lying on and wiggle my tingling fingers. I'm a little impressed she remembered. "Oh yeah. This guy's a badass."

After spending the night by the water, enjoying every minute of the luxury, we wake up happier and more refreshed than either of us can remember. The sun reflects off Erin's hair as she tilts her head back, laughing. "What's his name?"

"Shadow."

"Ooh, creepy. What makes him so evil?"

"I guess you'll just have to read the book to find out," I say, running my fingers through her hair.

"I want to read all your books," she says, growing sober. "I want to read the others' books too. I feel like I've lost half my life not doing what I love. You all inspire me so much."

"Hey, it doesn't matter when you start. You're starting now, that's what counts."

"Yeah, yeah, that's what they say. It doesn't change the way I feel about it." She starts to roll away, but I catch her with my free arm, not caring that my fingers on my other hand are going numb beneath her.

"Your book is going to be brilliant." I stare into her eyes, soaking up every ounce of the forest-green depths. "Your experiences make you the writer you are and who knows, if you had a happier life maybe you'd be kind of boring."

I chuckle as she swats at me, wiggling her way free. I chase her to the water, where we both dive in again and spend the rest of the morning without a care in the world.

HOURS PASS and the sun moves above us. We loathe the idea of leaving the lake after going so long without a reliable source of water. This is the true paradise we came here for and both of us want to soak up every ounce.

Eventually, we understand that we have to keep going, no matter how much we don't want to. We can't stay here forever. And the longer it takes us to get our act together, the more likely we are to be stuck here for good.

"All we need now is some meat," I say once the water bottles are filled and we're on our way.

"We need to try again for crabs."

My mouth waters at the thought. This isn't the first time we've talked about catching them, but so far, it hasn't happened yet, despite our best efforts. Every time she says the word, I picture a giant crab with fat, tender legs, waiting for me to crack it open. I almost groan at the image. "As soon as we get to the beach. They're active in the mornings."

"I don't think I'll ever eat another banana or mango for the rest of my life."

"Yeah, you can say that again. When we get out of here, I'm cutting fruit out of my diet."

We laugh together, neither of us giving words to what we both know. *There might not be an out of here.* Erin looks over her shoulder at me. "Maybe we should just stay on this side for a while. Until we figure a plan out, I mean."

I clear my throat before answering. "Yeah, we could do that. The water is closer, for sure. We should probably camp on the beach though." Just as the words leave my mouth, we step foot onto the sand. Where it was beautiful on the other side, over here it is gorgeous.

White sand stretches into the horizon, along with abandoned tiki umbrellas and lounge chair after lounge chair. It's almost identical to the other side, but the view, unblocked by the cliffside, is lit by the sunset.

"Andrew was right," Erin says. "There's a bathroom." She points to a small cement structure near the loungers. It looks to be crumbling like it's been abandoned for years. Interesting how the chairs and umbrellas look almost new.

"Looks that way."

"You think there was more to it than he said?"

"Yeah, I think there's a lot our *friend* wasn't telling us."

"Come on. Let's see if we can find anything useful."

We make our way down the seemingly endless beach, stopping every now and then to examine the lounge chairs. Erin thinks there might be things left behind underneath them—I don't, but I indulge her. She investigates the crumbling bathroom facilities, finds nothing.

"I think there has to be more to the story than what Andrew said. Would a cruise line really just abandon an island like this?" she says while searching.

"He didn't come back for us, so I don't really know what to think. Everything he said could be a lie."

"Exactly. I think so too."

"Does it really matter though? We know there's no one here. At least, on the parts of the island we've been."

"It matters because what if this island wasn't owned by a cruise line at all? Knowing *who* actually owns it might tell us why Andrew didn't come back for us, or might give us an idea of what they want with us."

"Maybe he doesn't want anything. Maybe this is just a sick joke to him."

"We have to keep looking. If I'm going to die here, I need to know for sure."

"Erin—"

"Come on. Let's keep going."

CHAPTER THIRTY-THREE

IT'S A CLEAR NIGHT, no storm in sight. The stars are amazing, the air cool against my chapped, burned skin. We moved some of the lounge chairs together to make a bed, just like when we camped out with the others.

I could get used to this. I smile, looking down at the top of Erin's head lying on my chest. "How long do you think we should stay here?" she asks.

My eyes are starting to droop. I force them open before saying, "As long as you want."

"Do you think they're really expecting to hear back from us?"

"They might start to worry if they don't hear something eventually—if they haven't wound up following us. I'm sure they think we'd leave without them if given the chance."

She tilts her head back to meet my gaze. "I'm not sure who we can trust."

"We don't have to trust any of them. All we have to do is get off this island and get back to the world."

She nods and turns back over.

A branch cracks in the distance.

Everything in my body freezes, down to my heart. I hold my breath, waiting to see if it was my imagination.

Erin does the opposite. She sits up instantly and stares into the darkness with wide eyes. "Tell me you heard that," she whispers.

"Yeah."

She gulps, digging her fingers into my arm so hard I can almost feel her breaking the skin. I wince at the pain but let her hold on. We both stare into the night, waiting. Seconds pass and then— "There it is again!" Erin hisses.

A breaking sound in the forest. "Is it closer?"

"I can't tell."

As gently as I can, I pry her fingers from my arm. "Erin, I think we need to move."

"To *where*?" She looks around us. "There's no place else."

"We can go farther down the beach. If it's an animal—"

"What kind of animal?"

I wrap her in my arms, trying to provide any comfort I'm able. "I don't know, but let's not find out, yeah?"

Erin nods. "Yeah. Okay, right. Let's go."

We gather the water bottles and head down the shoreline, all the while constantly glancing into the looming forest. Anything could be out there watching us. *Anyone* could be, too.

After about twenty minutes of walking, we stop, now far away from the tiki umbrellas and beach chairs. We settle down together on the sand, and while we both pretend to fall asleep, we're listening. It's so hard to tell over the sound of the waves, the palm leaves rustling in the wind, and my own beating heart, but I'm mostly sure we're alone again.

My own breaths even out with Erin's, and soon I'm drifting off, telling myself I didn't see the figure standing at the edge of the tree line watching us.

"GRAHAM, WAKE UP," Erin says next to my ear. She's talking between her teeth, shaking my shoulder, almost hissing at me like a cat.

I shield my eyes from the rays of sun and try to reorient myself but something's wrong, and Erin doesn't have the time or patience for me to wake up properly. "What's wrong?" I ask, half yawning. She dangles something above me. I blink away the sleep. It's a crab. I look at Erin, momentarily stunned. "How—"

She grins like the Cheshire cat. "You ready for breakfast?"

"I SAW SOMEONE. It wasn't an animal," Erin says between bites.

I lick my fingers, savoring every last bite of crab meat. The protein fills every ounce of me, rejuvenating me down to my soul. I almost feel like a new man from this meal alone.

"Did you recognize them?" I ask.

She shakes her head. "No. I saw movement in the trees, a definite outline, but that's all. I can't tell who it is."

Finished with my share of the crab, I stretch, casually looking in the direction she's indicating. "They could be gone now."

"Or not."

"Or not," I agree. I move my lips from side to side,

thinking about our situation. "Let's get off the beach. We're out in the open here, sitting ducks. If it's one of the others needing help or something, we'll see what's up."

"What about the gunshot? What if they don't need help but they're going to take care of us the way they took care of Tom?" Her voice is starting to rise with panic. This isn't the Erin I met on the cruise. She's losing herself to the situation and needs to pull it together.

"Hey," I say, putting a hand on her shoulder. "We're a team. We got this. I think your brain is in the perfect place to write a horror novel." I grin. "Maybe we should cowrite something."

She chuckles. "Yeah, right."

"Seriously though, both of our imaginations can be playing tricks on us. It could be a crooked tree out there or a bird flapping around making us go crazy."

Erin bites her lower lip and glances toward the tree line.

I continue, "If it is someone crazy, then at least we won't be so vulnerable. We'll have some cover off the beach."

"I'm not sure," she says. Then, "We still need to explore the rest of the beach."

I arch an eyebrow at her. "For?"

"I thought we were on the same page here."

"We were—we are. But we're over here now and there's nothing. I thought the goal was to see if there was civilization or a way out and there's neither of those things."

"We found water."

"Yeah, back in the forest."

"There's still miles of shoreline. Look—" She points in the distance. "The island wraps around again. There might be something over there."

I let out a deep sigh, trying not to insult her but I'm probably failing miserably. "Are we really going to walk the entire length of the island?"

"I mean, why not? Do you have something better to do?" She throws up her arms, exasperated. "We're *lost*! Stranded! Left for dead, for crying out loud, Graham. Don't you want to get the hell off this rock as bad as I do?"

"Of course I do—"

"Are you sure? Because you're starting to sound a lot like Marcella." She glares at me until I have to look away from the weight of it.

"You're right. I'm sorry. Let's at least refill the water bottles then we can keep going. If there is someone watching us, he hasn't hurt us yet. We'll figure it out when we need to. Is that the plan?"

Erin flattens her lips at the mention of the possible interloper but then she nods. "Yeah. I think we need to not let whoever this is stop us."

"Okay. I'm with you all the way. Let's get these bottles refilled." I brush the sand off myself, grab the bottles, and head toward the tree line.

CHAPTER THIRTY-FOUR

WE'VE BEEN WALKING for hours. Everything looks the same, but it doesn't seem to matter. Dread rises in me with each step we take. It's one of those unavoidable, looming sensations where you know something is going to go wrong.

Erin can't keep her eyes off the tree line. Every few minutes, she turns to scan before facing forward again. We were successful in filling up the bottles with fresh water—no further indication of someone else nearby. It's not enough for her though. She still feels the eyes on us.

We both pretend to ignore it, but we've also grown so accustomed to each other that we can read each other's emotions like a book. Something is off—it's just not quite clear what exactly, yet.

The island has another bend that we follow around and that's when we gasp in unison. The image of the white beach, green trees, and blue sky now has a different element. "Tell me you see it too," Erin says.

"Oh, I see it." In the sky, black smoke rises. Someone is burning a fire in the distance.

She starts to cry. "Graham, we're saved." Then she starts to run.

"Erin, wait a minute!" I call after her, trying to keep up but I'm not a runner like she is. She keeps going toward the smoke, following the beach until we run into another cliff edge.

Erin stops, considers the same problem we had days ago. She turns to me, half panicked, half crazed. "Where's the flare gun?"

"Hang on a minute, let's think about this," I pant, trying to catch my breath. I rack my brain for something to say to stop her, something that will make sense.

"Think about what? There's someone over there, probably looking for us! We need to shoot the flare. Now. This is what we've been waiting for—the reason we have *no fire*, the reason we haven't shot them!"

"Five minutes ago, we were worried about a stalker out there. How do we know this isn't him drawing us out?"

"It's not."

"How can you be sure?"

"Why didn't he do it before? I think we were just being a little paranoid. This is totally different." Erin reaches her hand toward me. "Give me the flare gun."

"I can't do that."

She sucks in a breath. "Graham."

"I'm sorry, Erin." I shake my head, defeated by the look she's giving me. "We need to stop for the night, gather our wits."

"Gather our wits? What the hell?"

I can hear her teeth grinding from where I stand. I'm not sure what to say to defuse the situation—we're clearly at odds and she's on the verge of her breaking point. I search for something else to say then she lunges for me.

She catches me off guard, her fingernails scratching deep into my skin when she reaches for me. I whip around, trying to get her to let go. When I do, she punches my back, arms, and stomach. One of her hits lands just over my lungs.

I gasp for air, desperate not to hurt her but it's the only way to make her stop. "Erin," I say. She doesn't hear me. She keeps coming at full force, trying to get to the flare gun.

"Give it to me!" she screams. Her fingertips brush against the gun in my back pocket.

I shove against her chest, pushing as hard as I can. Erin stumbles backward, almost falls but catches herself. She lunges again and this time I swing, hating myself for doing it, but it's the only way.

My fist connects with her shoulder with a deep thud. She cries out in pain and outrage, but she's still not stopping. I swing at her again.

She falls to the sand, crying. "Graham, don't do this. This is what we've been waiting for!"

"I'm sorry, Erin. I can't let you shoot that flare."

"Why are you so against it? Are you that afraid?"

I walk away from her, unwilling to answer. *Unable to.* I open and close my fist, sore from hitting her. Guilt fills me to the brim to the point I can't look at her.

I keep walking in the opposite direction, hoping she'll stop, knowing she won't. She's running behind me. I brace myself, twisting at the last second.

Erin isn't reaching for me, though. She body-slams into me with her full strength and momentum, bringing us both down. She headbutts me before I have a chance to react. My nose is broken. I scream as blood spills down my face and fills my mouth.

She hurt herself too, but she still has the upper hand. In a swift motion, she grabs the flare gun from my pocket, points it into the sky, and shoots. A flare soars into the sky, popping like a firework.

"We have to get out of here," I say, trying to wipe the blood from my face. I reach for her, but she pulls away.

"No."

"Erin, please. You don't understand."

A look of confusion passes over her. "What aren't you telling me?"

"Nothing. Just—we have to get out of here."

"That's what I've been trying to do!"

"No, goddammit! Out of this spot. As far away as we can get." I reach for her again, this time grabbing hold of her arm. Instead of staying on the beach, I lead her toward the tree line.

"Stop!" Erin cries, pulling back. She struggles, but I won't let her go. "We're going the wrong way! The smoke is that way!"

I don't speak. There's no time. The only thing that matters now is getting as far away as we can.

PART 5

WADE

CHAPTER THIRTY-FIVE

THE RAIN KEEPS MAKING our hands slip on the raft. Caleb won't slow down, which is only making it worse. "Hurry the hell up," he barks at me over his shoulder.

"My hands keep slipping, man. It's too steep here. We need to take it easy for a minute."

"Stop being such a pussy, Wade." He yanks the logs forward, trying to pull me along with them, but instead they fall from my hands completely. Our section of raft is too heavy for Caleb to carry on his own, so when my end falls, his does too.

The logs hit the ground and break apart, rolling all over the place. Caleb screams, furious with me for not hanging on, furious with himself for screwing up. We stand facing each other, trying to catch our breath, when there's movement behind us.

Caleb and I turn to see Andrew watching us with a gun pointed in our direction. Our jaws drop. "You came back," I say.

"I'm going to kill you, asshole!" Caleb screams.

Andrew shakes his head, points the gun at Caleb. "You

might want to adjust your tone. I need to speak with the both of you but I'm not going to unless you can be calm."

Caleb takes a step back, looks between us, and whispers, "Wait a minute... is he... you know—" He motions between us. "Part of this too?"

"He knows," Andrew says.

"The ship wasn't supposed to leave! We weren't supposed to be left like this!" Caleb bursts out.

"I told you you'd be on an abandoned island. What did you think that meant?"

"You said it would be like reality TV for writers—"

"Is this not reality enough for you?" Andrew smirks. "And still no fire? I can't say I'm very impressed."

Caleb's lips flatten together as his jaw tightens. He's barely controlling his temper by a thread. Andrew's attitude is going to push him over any second. I look at Caleb in a new light, everything starting to make a little more sense now. He seems to do the same to me. "So why are you here?" I ask Andrew. "You said the only rule was to not tell anyone else, not talk about it at all. I haven't done those things. I'm guessing Caleb hasn't either."

"I'm here because I want someone to tell me what the fuck you all are up to and where Graham and Erin are." He lifts his eyebrows, waiting for one of us to come up with a good response. When we take too long to answer, he kicks at a piece of the fallen section of the raft. "Answer me, goddammit!"

"We're building a raft," Caleb says.

"Why?"

"To get out of here."

"And—" Andrew strokes his chin. "Was that part of the plan?"

"We didn't know what else to think," I say. "We're playing

the part. That's what you wanted, and we haven't been in contact. It's been days, weeks."

"You were hired to do a job and you're not doing it." Andrew glares at us, finger stroking the gun barrel. "I told you to play along, not to escape."

"We are absolutely doing it. We are playing the part you wanted us to play. Wouldn't it look funny if we all laid back and relaxed, did nothing to *try*?"

"And what are you going to do when it's time to actually set sail?"

"I'll take care of that," Caleb says.

"I thought the idea was not to stay here forever," I say carefully. "What's wrong with setting out on the raft after a while?"

"The idea is for you to not fucking question when I say something," Andrew says. "I'm not the one who sets the rules. You know that. And you're getting paid enough money to keep your mouth shut. That was the agreement, yeah?"

My lips press into a fine line. I nod. "Yeah, Andrew."

"Good. And by the way, plans change, and you need to be able to roll with the dice. Is that clear?"

"Crystal."

"Now, some good news. Since Tom has passed, his paycheck is available to be split between you."

Caleb and I look at each other, shocked. *Tom was in on it too? Who the hell else is?* For all we know, we could all be. And if they're giving us his share, what will they do if something happens to one of us? They'll most likely give the other survivor more money.

"Since neither of you has anything to say about that..." Andrew says, "Where are Graham and Erin, and when will they be back?"

Caleb and I exchange another look. "They're not down

the beach anymore?" Caleb asks. "I thought you had cameras everywhere."

Andrew scowls. "Reception has been—spotty lately." His irritation with us is growing exponentially, and it's not clear what he'll do about it. With his connections, he can probably get away with anything he damn well wants, so it's best for us not to push him too far when he has us cornered like this.

"They wanted to make it to the other side of the cliff," I say. "They said they're looking for another source of water and any other way we might get off the island."

Andrew strokes his chin again, thinking. "Any ideas on when they'll be back?"

"Maybe a couple more days. No way to know for sure unless we get over there first." I almost shift under his scrutiny, but I force myself to stay still.

Andrew nods. "Alright then. I'll leave you all to it."

"Hang on a sec," Caleb says. "Please tell me you have some food with you. Or some water bottles or a damn lighter. We're dying here." He holds out his hands in a pleading gesture.

Andrew gives a tight smile. "Sorry, friend. Wish I could help but if the others saw, it would be game over."

"They won't see!" Caleb starts to raise his voice again, on the verge of panic.

Footsteps are running toward us now—Marcella and Lauren. How much have they heard? Are they in on this too? If they're not, what will Andrew do to them? They come down off the hill to see the three of us. "Graham?" Lauren says. "Where's Erin?"

Andrew turns to look at them. "I'd like to know the same thing," he says before pointing a gun at her and blowing a hole through her head.

My ears are ringing. I try to blink but can't seem to. We

stand frozen, staring at Lauren's so-called *friend*, each of us afraid to move even a muscle. Wisps of smoke float from the gun barrel into the air. Lauren lies dead at our feet, her blood pooling around her, soaking into the ground.

I look to Marcella, who has her hands over her mouth to keep from screaming. A small moan escapes between her fingers. Specks of Lauren's blood are on her face and hands, but she doesn't notice.

I look to Caleb, who looks more relieved than shocked. His expression surprises me, but it also explains why she seemed to be afraid of him the last few days.

Finally, I turn back to Andrew, who's assessing all of us, waiting for a reaction. "Are we going to have a problem here?" he asks.

Caleb and I shake our heads without hesitation, but Marcella is frozen still.

"Marcella?" Andrew asks.

She shakes her head.

"Good."

"You're—you're not going to take us home?" she asks.

"I'm afraid not." He shakes his head, gives a shrug then leaves us without another word, taking a path that none of us noticed before, back into the thick of the trees.

CHAPTER THIRTY-SIX

"What did he say to you and why is he after Erin?" Tears run down Marcella's cheeks. She can't stop staring at Lauren's body, sprawled across the forest floor, blood still draining into the earth.

"He—didn't say anything," I say, trying to look away. My stomach doesn't like the sight. "He just wanted to know where they were, didn't say why."

Her eyes flash. "That's bullshit." She turns to Caleb. "We heard you yelling. That's why Lauren came running first. She thought you were going to do something and wanted to get here to try stopping you."

"I don't know what she thought I would do." He looks angry at the accusation, offended that Lauren would even think something like that. "I was—angry. Andrew had the gun, and he refused to take us home—"

"Why aren't we following him? He has to have a boat. What the hell is going on here?"

"Remember the gun? He shot Lauren without a second thought. He'll do the same to us if he needs to."

She looks at both of us, thinking. Then she says, "He didn't say anything? Why he's doing this to us? *Nothing?*"

"Nothing," I say, frowning. "Trust me, we tried to get answers out of him, but we'd rather be lost here than shot to death."

The way Marcella is looking at us—it's obvious she doesn't trust us. I don't like the cold gleam in her eyes, the way she's thinking about *us* instead of taking what we say at face value. She's putting too much thought into it, which isn't good.

I don't understand why Andrew shot Lauren and not Marcella. Lauren is the reason we're here—if anything, he owed her a thank-you instead of a bullet. Marcella bends down to Lauren now, holding her hand as she says goodbye. Then she stands and says, "Who's going to help me carry my section?"

"Leave it. We'll come back for it when it's time to get more water," Caleb says. "We can put Lauren next to Tom, too." We still don't have a way to carry any water, not more than will drain out of a canvas backpack, anyway. We'll be going back soon enough.

He and I gather our scattered section of the raft into a pile, each taking an end, and we all continue on to the beach.

WE'RE a little better off than starting from scratch, but this time seems to go faster now that we have the wood and other supplies already gathered. We spend the rest of the day at our old camp on the beach, finishing the first section of the raft, with plans to go back tomorrow for the rest of the scattered section and for Lauren's body.

Caleb sits beside me on the sand while I work. "Do you think they'll kill us?" he asks.

"No."

"What makes you so certain?"

"What reason do they have? We're doing what they want."

"They don't need a reason, do they?"

"We're as guilty as they are. If they killed all their employees, they would have no one left, and it's easier to keep those who are reliable, who they know will keep doing it."

"Would you keep doing it?"

"If I have to."

He nods in understanding. We're all here for one reason and one reason only. Money. The bigger your need, the more you're willing to do to get your hands on it.

"What about Graham and Erin? Do you think they'll kill them? Or want one of us to do it?"

I pull the binding too tight around the logs, making it snap. At the same time, my jaw is clenched so tight my teeth grind together.

"Jeez, take it easy," Caleb says.

"I think they probably will, yeah."

We stare at each other for a second without speaking, each understanding that we have to do what we have to do, even if we don't like it. Our beds are made, and it's time to lie in them.

"You think Graham and Erin will find any water over on that side?"

I shrug. "Maybe. Does it really matter?"

"I guess you're right."

"Are you two ever going to stop flirting and do your part?" Marcella calls from the other end of the logs. She's watching us warily like we're keeping a secret from her. That's pretty much exactly what we're doing but it still stings to have her looking at us like that. *At least she's not trying to come onto me anymore.*

We work in silence until the section is complete and we're ready to go back for the rest.

THE THREE OF us sit side by side on the sand, looking at the completed raft. It's stronger now than before. We tested it to make sure it wouldn't fall apart this time.

On the edge of the shoreline, it sits, waiting for us to push it far enough in the water to be carried away. Caleb's job is to stop that from happening when the time comes. My job is to convince everyone else that we're trying our hardest to get off this rock—not exactly a lie.

"Looks great," Caleb says. "You think it'll actually float?"

"It better. After seeing Andrew—I think it's about our last hope left." Marcella says.

"It'll work," I say, filling my voice with determination.

We spend the night with rumbling stomachs under the same old familiar shelter, agreeing to allow a few more nights before we set out down the beach in search of Erin and Graham.

CHAPTER THIRTY-SEVEN

THERE's movement during the night, but I'm too tired to care about it. Whoever is up to something can go on their merry way because I am too damned tired, weak, and hungry to give a shit. *How does Andrew expect us to do what we need to do without food?*

I fall back asleep, ignoring the sounds until Caleb's yelling wakes me up again. "No, no, no! Fuck!" He runs to me, shaking me like his life depends on waking me up. "Wade! Fuck, wake up!"

"What's going on?" I sit up to see him looking at me half crazed.

"That bitch! God, they're gonna kill us!"

"Marcella? What happened? Where is she?" I stand up now and move out from under the shelter. That's when I see what he's so pissed about. I run my hands through my hair, impressed by her bold move but growing just as worried as Caleb.

"You see now?" he says.

"Yeah. I see." Marcella used high tide to push the raft into the ocean. And she left without us. She made it past the breaker and is on her way to the open ocean. There's nothing we can do to stop her.

"What are we gonna do? We can't let her get away —can we?"

"I don't think Andrew wanted that, no. But I don't see what we can do now."

"Fuck!" Caleb throws his hands in the air and starts walking around in circles with frantic motions. He's going off the rails, no longer in control. "I can't die here. This was supposed to be easy, straightforward. That fucking bitch! Why'd she have to do that?"

"Hey," I say, trying to calm him down. "She might die out there."

"No, that doesn't matter. Andrew didn't care when you brought that up before." He waves me off while continuing to walk around the beach and mumbles to himself. Suddenly he stops. Caleb turns and looks at me with renewed interest, like he's had a brilliant idea.

Dread works its way down my spine from the look on his face. "What is it?"

He takes a step toward me. "They want us to kill each other."

"Whoa, hang on. I don't think that's—"

He takes another step. "Of course it is. Why else would Andrew mention the money—the *splitting* of the dead man's money?"

I start to back away from him. There's no way I want any part of this. Caleb has actually lost his last marble and I could curse Marcella for leaving me alone with him. "Caleb, they don't want us to kill each other."

"What makes you so sure?"

"They just wanted entertainment—"

"Exactly!" he screams, eyes nearly bulging out of his face. In a flurry, he turns and runs to the shelter.

I hear a zipper. He's rummaging through something, and the seconds are ticking down. Now's the time. *What's it gonna be, Wade?*

There's not going to be another chance, and I don't know how much time I have left. With careful, precise movements, I step farther away from Caleb and the shelter, toward the tree line. I keep moving until I know I'm far enough away to run.

"Wade?" he calls, unable to see me now that I'm hidden.

I watch him search for me, a pocketknife in his hand. *How in the hell did he get that? God, that would've come in handy!* Andrew wanted entertainment? Well, I hope his cameras are getting a good view of this action because this is about as real as it gets. There's no doubt in my mind what Caleb plans to do with that knife.

"Come on, Wade, I was just messin' around," Caleb calls. He turns to look in my direction, and for a moment, my heart stutters when I think he sees me. He starts to approach, holding the knife behind his back like I'm an idiot who doesn't know what he's trying to do.

"Hey, man, we gotta stop fuckin around and get going," he says. "We need to go get Erin and Graham, show Andrew we can set things straight."

He's almost on me now, so close I can smell his sweat. He passes me. And I take the chance, jumping at him with a vine wrapped around my fists. I swing it over his head and around his throat, holding it as tight as I can.

He struggles to free himself, reaching up with the knife to cut the vine. His blade is small, but it works. He's able to make a small incision, and with the pressure, it doesn't take long for the vine to break.

Caleb clutches his throat, glaring at me. "You tried to kill me!"

"Same." I nod to the knife he's still holding.

He takes a second to catch his breath, then charges at me without another word. I try to dodge the knife but I'm no fighter. He slices my forearm open—not deep but enough to make blood stain the sand.

He's on the offense, swiping, stabbing, lurching. Sweat beads on his forehead with the effort. Somehow, I manage to keep dodging his frantic attacks, backing myself toward the water. It feels like hours, we're both drained, but there's nothing else for it. One of us is going to die.

My feet touch the water, and I can almost breathe a sigh of relief. I keep walking farther out, luring him, until we can walk no farther. I start to swim, knowing he won't be able to use the knife anymore.

"Where are you going?" Caleb says. "There's nowhere to go." He starts to laugh. "Think you can catch up with Marcella, huh?"

Actually no, but not a bad idea. I don't answer. I focus all my energy on swimming, on outsmarting him. The waves are getting bigger. It's getting harder to keep my head above water when they come.

I can hear Caleb coughing behind me when he swallows a mouthful of ocean. Hope swells in my chest. *Maybe he'll tire himself out and drown without me laying a finger on him.*

The distance between us grows, but I keep going until I'm sure Caleb is spent. He treads water, half-floating, half just trying to keep his nose above the water. "Hey, are there sharks out here?" he asks.

"Probably."

He snickers. "Wouldn't that be something? We both get eaten."

I don't answer, and he doesn't seem to mind. I watch him, waiting, making sure he's not going to surprise me. Then, when I'm completely sure, I swim toward him to end it.

Just like I'd hoped, he dropped the knife while swimming. He puts up a fight, but I was right to think he was done. Caleb doesn't have enough energy left. He goes under and doesn't come back up.

CHAPTER THIRTY-EIGHT

THERE'S ONLY one thing left for me to do—find Graham and Erin. I spend time gathering what supplies I can, what supplies I'm willing to carry, and set out down the beach. I have a few drops of water I can squeeze from the canvas bag and there's one rotten banana left. I'm not sure how long it'll take me to reach them, but I sure as hell hope they found water. Because if they didn't, things are going to get ugly.

IT TAKES hours to make my way down the beach. As I walk, I keep wondering if they would've gone inland versus staying near the water. I'm hoping I'm right in assuming their train of thought, but what if I'm wrong? It could take me forever to find them.

Luckily, I soon discover that I'm not wrong. By night, I've reached a spot that I believe is where they're camping or have camped. There are signs of their presence everywhere.

Instead of calling out for them, I decide to wait and save my breath and energy. I hear neither Graham nor Erin's voice and decide they're not here. It's just a matter of if they're coming back or if they've moved on. My gut says they've moved, especially since they wanted to get over the cliff, but I decide to stick around for the night.

In the morning, they still haven't shown so I follow my instinct and keep moving. I move inland to the forest and find the path they left behind. I finally breathe a sigh of relief. *I'm going to find them after all.*

COMING down from the other side is like opening the door to a whole new world. This side of the island takes my breath away. *It's almost like leveling up.* I feel ridiculous for thinking it but can't help comparing our situation to a video game.

Now that I'm downhill, I tread more carefully. I have no way of knowing if something happened to Graham or Erin or what kinds of predators might be lurking. It's best to keep as silent as possible for now.

I keep moving, feeling my hunger and thirst with every breath I take. My lips are dry, the inside of my mouth feels like sandpaper. I'm consumed by the need to drink, so much that I can hardly think of anything else.

I try to focus on my purpose—finding the others. *They'll have water. They'll have food. Everything will be fine. Why did I agree to this again?* That's not even a question, really. Why does anyone do anything stupid when money is involved? Because they're desperate for it. That's why.

My credit card debt up to my eyeballs, late fees, looming

collection agencies, and depleted credit score need this money. I remind myself *it's worth being a little thirsty to get out from under it.* Not only that, but the marketing possibilities for my books with all that money.

I stop when I hear a sound. It's something out of the ordinary, so faint I almost miss it. I fight against the dizziness, trying to concentrate. *What was it?*

There it is again! I turn in the direction it came from, my heart racing. *Please don't let me be dreaming!*

Splashing. The sound of sweet, sweet water reaches my ears. If I had any saliva left in me, I'd be drooling.

I quicken my pace, suddenly desperate to reach the liquid gold, frantic to find that I'm not dreaming after all. Almost as an afterthought, I realize that splashing means someone else is there too. I don't really care, though. Nothing is getting in the way of me and that water.

When I finally reach the clearing, I give myself five seconds to check my surroundings, check the water to make sure it's real and not going to kill me, then I drink my fill. It tastes so good I could almost weep. Eventually I force myself to stop so I don't get sick, and that's when I dunk my entire head under the surface, relishing the cool balm against my chapped skin.

When I'm finally done, finally full and satisfied and cooled down, I feel like I could sleep for a year. I assess my surroundings again. It had to be them splashing but there's no one here now. Did I really *just* miss them by that much? It could've been some kind of wild animal.

For now, I'm going to sleep for a few hours. If it was Graham and Erin—they're close. And I'll find them when I wake up.

WHEN I WAKE UP, it's pitch black, the only light coming from the moon and stars. I have no shelter, no cover. I play with the idea of moving. Is it safer here? Then I think of the animals. This could be their only source of water, and who knows what will come looking for a drink in the night.

My mind made up, I get moving. I head in the direction the waves seem the loudest, not so much searching for Graham and Erin, but believing it's probably the safest place to spend the night. To my immense relief, it doesn't take me long.

And there they are. *Lying in each other's arms.* There are lounge chairs and umbrellas just like on the other side. Graham and Erin moved them together to make a cozy little place to screw.

I look away in disgust. *Cameras pick up all that, too?* No doubt. I try to shake off the disappointment but it's hard. I thought there might've been something—no, of course not. She's only a lonely divorcée looking for affection from the first man willing to give it. Nothing else.

I wander off, but not far. I'm just taking a look around while they're—busy. I keep going, no longer as worried about predators. Now, my biggest concern is drowning out the noises they're making. My stomach heaves. I keep going until I hear no more.

After a while, when things go quiet, I make my way back to them, ready to make myself known. I think about how I should do it. I could just pop out, say, "Hi guys!" or I could wait until morning, acting like I've been walking all night—not untrue.

A fallen branch cracks beneath my foot. I flinch at the noise. Erin and Graham heard it too. They're both looking in my direction with frightened faces. *Now's my chance. Make yourself known, Wade.*

Something stops me. I don't want to be the creep who's watching them, but I can't just pop out like I wasn't doing that all along. No, I decide, I'll wait until morning.

They start to move farther down the beach, and I almost laugh. *Do they really think that's going to save them?* If I really was a predator, that would do nothing to deter me.

I keep pace with them, staying out of sight behind the tree line until they stop again for the night. I make myself cozy and wait for the sun to rise.

PART 6

ERIN

CHAPTER THIRTY-NINE

GRAHAM WON'T LET GO of my arm. I'm trying to free myself of his grip, but he only tightens it with each move I make. "Knock it off," he says, yanking me forward.

"You're hurting me!" I cry.

"I can't let you go over there." He ducks under a low-lying branch and dodges around limbs in our way. Palm leaves smack my face, there's no time to evade them all.

"I don't understand. What do you know that I don't?"

"Nothing. But I do know after hearing someone out there watching us and then seeing smoke the next morning—running to it isn't the smartest thing. We can't just draw them to us, either. We have to be smart."

I let myself fall to the ground, pulling him to an abrupt stop. Pain rips through my shoulder and elbow at the tension but it's worth it to see the look on his face. "I don't care if it's Satan himself over there. I'm getting off this island."

Graham stares at me, out of breath, disbelieving. "They could be here to kill us."

I scoff. "Really, Graham? Who the hell would be here to do that? They could just leave us to starve."

Movement comes from behind us. Graham struggles to yank me up—I'm doing everything I can to fight him, to slow him down.

"Over here!" I call.

Just as he gets me over his shoulder, someone says, "Let her go."

The voice sounds familiar—someone we know who's come to help, not some crazy axe murderer like Graham suggested. I try to see who it is but am only able to see Graham's back. I kick and squirm, giving Graham a hell of a time but he hangs on through all my attempts. "You heard him. Let me go!"

"You're not going anywhere with him," Graham says. He turns to continue walking. I lift up as much as I'm able and that's when I see Wade.

He meets my gaze and holds a finger to his lips. Then he comes at full speed, his momentum throwing Graham off balance. The three of us fall in a heap and finally, Graham loosens his grip.

I scramble to get away while their fists fly at each other's faces. I make it a few feet away but they come too close in their fight, so I back away farther. I gasp when I see that Graham has Wade in a headlock. Wade's trying to get out of it but doesn't seem able to.

"Stop!" I yell. "That's enough!"

He doesn't listen. He stays in the same position with his arm around Wade's neck. Wade's face is starting to turn purple. *If I don't do something, he's going to kill him.*

I charge at Graham, shoving him hard enough for Wade to get out from under him. It's also enough for him to get the upper hand. When Graham is off balance from the push, Wade kicks his feet out from under him and now has the advantage.

This isn't what I wanted at all. I'm not trying to take sides —I just want them to stop. "Wade! Stop!" I move to step between them but they're so close it's impossible for me to squeeze in.

I scream at the top of my lungs, a high-pitched cry that makes the birds fly from the treetops. Wade finally looks at me, startled, like he's seeing me for the first time. He backs away from Graham with his hands in the air. "I'm done," he says.

"Thank God."

"He was hurting you, Erin."

I'm not sure if he was or wasn't, but whatever he did, it didn't register this kind of violence. "I'm fine," I say. "Thank you for coming." I go to Graham's side to make sure he's still breathing.

His breaths are ragged, he might have a broken rib, but he'll live. I try to help wipe some of the blood off his face, but he grabs my arm to stop me. "Please don't go with him," he whispers so only I can hear.

"Why not?"

"I don't trust him. After everything—"

"Is it because of what just happened?"

"No—it's because—"

"Is he going to live?" Wade interrupts.

Graham's fists clench at his side. "I'll be fine."

"Good. Now, Erin, we should get going."

I look between them, shocked he would leave Graham alone and in this condition, but also torn because I'm not sure if it's the right thing to do. I'm not going to let Graham stop me from getting off the island and it seems that's exactly what he wants to do. If he's not willing to ask strangers to save us, I'm not sure how he expects to get off this damned rock.

They're both bloodied but Graham seems almost broken.

He still hasn't sat up. "I can't leave him like this," I say to Wade. "He can't even sit up."

"Yes, I—" Graham starts but moans in pain when he tries.

"See?" I look at Graham carefully. "You're coming with us and you're not going to stop us."

He shakes his head. "Don't do this."

"I don't know how you can say that. It would be insane for us to ignore someone here on the island with a potential way out. Are you in or what?"

He nods.

"And you won't try to stop us?"

"Not physically, anyway."

I look toward Wade. "You two won't kill each other, will you?"

He holds up his hands. "I can control myself."

"Can you though?"

He has the decency to blush. "I can. I promise."

"Okay, then help me get him up." When Graham is up and stable and has an arm wrapped around each of us, we set out.

CHAPTER FORTY

THERE ARE SO many questions I have for Wade. It seems like it's been a year since Graham and I set out away from the others. I want to know what they've been up to, if they've found any food or water, started a fire, or found a way out that we haven't thought of. I also want to know if they missed the bottles that Graham and I took, but I know that's something I won't be able to ask straight out. Mostly, what the hell is he doing over here?

"I assume we're headed toward that plume of smoke on the horizon?" Wade says. "I overheard a little of what you two were saying. You think there's someone here to rescue us?"

"Yeah, that's where we're going. And yeah, I think that but as you probably guessed, Graham and I are in a disagreement about it."

Wade's eyebrows shoot up. "That smoke has to be from someone else here on the island. What makes you think they're not willing to save us if we make it over there?"

Graham doesn't want to answer. I can tell he doesn't want to be anywhere near Wade, let alone explain himself. He's silent for a few seconds before saying, "I just don't trust it."

"We'll be careful," I say. "But we have to try."

He moves a few feet away from us. "I can walk on my own for a while," he says, looking away.

Now that we're going in the right direction, we're able to stay on the beach for a ways until it's time to cut through the trees. It saves us the headache of having to duck under branches every two feet or make sure no spiders drop down our backs. Plus, it makes it easier to help Graham. *When he'll let us help.*

"So, why did you leave camp anyway? And where are the others?" I ask Wade.

He takes a minute to answer and the longer he has to think about it the more concerned I become. *Is it that he's thinking of the right thing to say... or that the reason is too difficult to speak about?* Finally he says, "There was an accident."

I stop in my tracks, my heart in my throat. An accident. *Like Tom.* "What happened? Is everyone okay?"

"No. They're not."

"Why didn't you say something before? We have to go to them! What happened? How bad are they hurt?" Sweat breaks out on my forehead. I'm walking in circles now, torn between leaving everything to go to them and making them wait while we continue on to find help. They're hurt now too, plus Graham in his condition. My mind reels with the possibility of having another death on our hands.

"Hey, it's not like that," Wade says. He reaches out to touch my shoulder to hold me still. "No one is dying. They're not fine because Marcella sprained an ankle and won't stop complaining. Lauren is taking care of her while Caleb keeps them fed and watered."

I release a breath. Dizziness overcomes me, and I have to bend over to put my head between my knees. I force myself to calm down. "I'm sorry."

"No—I should've been clearer up front."

"Why didn't you stay with them and send Caleb?" Graham asks.

"Well... I volunteered." He blushes. "To be honest, I kind of needed some space from Marcella. She keeps—you know." His blush grows deeper as he rolls his eyes.

"Come on, let's keep moving," I say, standing back up.

We keep moving until we finally have no choice but to turn from the beach and enter the forest. Wade and I take turns helping Graham along, even when he insists he can manage. He walks fine, but it doesn't take long for him to start stumbling over everything, so it's easier just to help him to begin with.

When it's my turn to help, Graham whispers, "There's something wrong here, Erin."

"This again?"

He shakes his head. "No, I mean with Wade."

"What are you talking about?"

"He doesn't seem like the type of guy to leave everyone when they're down. His story just seems—off."

I think about what he's saying, and I suppose he could be right. But who are we to call him a liar? More importantly, *why* would he lie? What would be the point? "I don't think there's anything in it for him to lie to us...."

"There doesn't have to be. A psychopath needs no *reward*. They do what they do because it's what they want."

I almost step away from him while he's leaning on me to get over a fallen tree. I want to shove him away, to slap him for saying such a thing. "He's a psychopath now? Graham, listen to yourself,"

"I'm sorry, I didn't mean that, exactly. It's just—" He looks up ahead of us. Wade isn't far. "I wish you would listen to me here. You keep brushing off everything I'm saying. Just listen, damnit. Stop being so worried about getting to the smoke and take in the actual situation."

He's staring at me so intently, it's impossible not to take him seriously. "Okay," I say just as Wade turns to say, "You guys doing okay back there?"

Graham gives me a meaningful look and we catch up.

CHAPTER FORTY-ONE

AFTER A NIGHT of camping out in the forest, we wake up to find the smoke is gone. Whatever was burning isn't burning anymore and I can almost cry from the frustration. "Please tell me one of you knows which direction it was," I say, staring into the sky. It's hard to tell beneath the canopy of trees, but I'm somewhat sure I know which way to go.

Graham and Wade look up at the sky too. "I can still see wisps of it," Wade says. He points. "That way."

I turn in the direction he's indicated, focus, but can't seem to make out what he sees. "Are you sure?"

"Yeah. You don't see it?"

"I don't see anything either," Graham says. "And last night we were headed in that direction," he points the opposite way.

My spine starts to tingle. My palms grow damp and I wipe them dry across my pants. *It's okay. We're going to figure this out.*

I move around the both of them to look at our camp more closely. It was nearly dark when we stopped, and everything looks almost identical here. Even so, how can we not remember?

I'm no tracker, so I'm not really sure what I'm looking for. It's obvious where we slept—the ground is matted. "Help me look for our trail," I say.

They catch on quick and soon we find something that looks like where we might've come from. "Looks like neither of you had it quite right." I smile at them, trying to ease the tension.

IT TAKES the rest of the day before we're certain we haven't made a mistake. Since there's no more smoke, there's no indicator for us to follow. We keep going anyway, Wade leading the way most of the time, and eventually we smell the leftover smoke.

"We're close," Wade says, turning back to us.

When we start to smell old fire smoke, my heart races. I can see it on Graham's face too. We're close to the beach again, and it seems that's where the smell is coming from.

Wade pushes past one final tree and—my stomach drops out from under me.

"A—bonfire?" I say, trying to understand. There's no one here. The area is completely void of life, why would there be a random burned pile in the middle of the sand? "Hello!" I scream. "Hello! Is anyone here?" *Someone has to be nearby*.

"Where else would the smoke come from?" Graham says, back to the smart-ass I met on the ship.

I give him a look that makes him flinch. "An organized bonfire like this doesn't start itself. There's someone else here.

They can't be far." I barely have time to think about the luxury of having a fire. *Warmth at night, cooked food, light—If we could've just been a little sooner, we could've saved some of the embers if nothing else.*

"If they meant to help us, they would've waited," Graham says. Neither he nor Wade has called out for anyone. They're just accepting that there's no one here without even trying.

"What if they did wait and when no one showed, they took off?"

"Then—I guess they're gone."

My fists clench with the urge to sock him in the shoulder. I take a few steps away, searching, even though there's nowhere to search. Everything is wide open and clear here. There are no boats in the water, no people waiting in the sand. The only place left to go is back into the trees—where we just came from. I can't just give up now. I thought for sure following the smoke here would give us some kind of answer—thought it was a sign that someone was here. *How can this just be it?*

"Hello!" I call again, cupping my hands over my mouth in an effort to be louder. I turn back toward the guys. "We need to go back into the forest. Someone is here. They didn't just sail away. No way—I can't accept that."

"Hey, Erin?" Wade says.

"What?" I snap.

He's pointing back at the tree line. I follow his line of sight —and almost fall to my knees. Andrew—Lauren's friend from the cruise, is walking toward us.

CHAPTER FORTY-TWO

Tears spring to my eyes the moment I see him. I almost want to pinch myself to make sure he's real. A million questions spring to mind but the only thing I'm able to say is, "Thank God."

Andrew grins at me. He raises his arms in the air and says, "It's me, the one and only! Glad you saw my smoke signal."

"What took you so long? It's been weeks. We thought—well, it doesn't matter now. The others are on the other side of the island, where you first dropped us. We'll have to go back for them."

Andrew's grin widens. He looks at Wade. "Are they now?"

"That's right," Wade says.

"Is something wrong?" I ask, looking between them. I look to Graham and notice he's not exactly thrilled to see Andrew either. *There's something they all know that they're not telling me.*

"Should I tell her, or would one of you gentlemen like to do the honors?" Andrew says.

Dread grows in the pit of my stomach. "Tell me what?"

Andrew's amused smile makes me want to punch him in the face. Wade's look of worry makes me want to scream. But it's Graham's look of pure, unrestrained rage that makes me want to turn and run.

My eyes meet Graham's. "Andrew isn't here to save us, Erin," he says.

I look back to Andrew, shocked, unable to understand.

He shrugs, all innocence. "He's right."

My brow furrows. I'm trying to understand, but it seems to be escaping me. "I don't—what do you mean? If you're not here to help us, then why are you here? Why come back?"

Andrew smiles at me again, this time nodding toward Wade. "Why don't you ask your friend over there."

Wade is shaking his head, pleading with his eyes.

"Wade?" I say.

"Tell her," Andrew says.

"I lied," he says. "We—I'm pretty sure all of us lied. Or a few of us anyway."

"Okay... about what exactly? What does this have to do with getting off the island?"

"It has everything to do with it." He takes a step toward me. "This is all staged," he whispers.

"All—"

"They paid us to be here," Graham says.

I swing toward him. "You knew about it?"

"They both did," Andrew says, pleased with himself.

"I'm so confused." I run my hands through my hair and close my eyes to concentrate. "What's the point? Why tell me now? Why come back now? Why do this at all? I don't *get it*."

Andrew takes a few steps toward the closest tree. He motions for me to follow. Once I do, he points up to something on the tree trunk. At first, I don't see what he wants me to see, but I squint and focus and then— "Is that a—camera?"

"Bingo. A microcamera, camouflaged, they're hidden *everywhere*." He wiggles his eyebrows at me with a knowing look.

I feel myself turn scarlet. *They saw everything.* "We're being watched."

"From day one."

A feeling of faintness comes over me. "*Who* exactly is doing the watching?" The scarier question here is *why is he telling me now?* But I'm too frightened to ask.

Wade's and especially Graham's betrayal sit heavy on my chest, but I force myself to ignore it for now. I have to wrap my head around what's happening. I have a feeling that being trapped on this island wasn't the worst part of our situation. There's going to be something worse.

"There are investors," Andrew says. "The investors provide their audience with whom and what they'd like to see. I don't know who the audience is, but let's just say they're people with a lot of money."

"I wasn't asked if I wanted to be here. I wasn't given a choice. Why were they?"

Andrew shrugs. "That's just how it works. Some get a choice... some don't."

I want to protest, to demand he take this more seriously. His carefree attitude is starting to annoy the hell out of me. Something tells me it will do me no good though. He doesn't care if I want to be here or not. It never made a difference to him or whoever these *investors* are.

"So. They got their footage. We're here, stuck. You win." I throw my hands up. "What now?" *The million-dollar question.*

"Well, like any good show, it's all about the ratings, right? What's going to make the viewers jump out of their seats, screaming at the TV. What's going to make them enjoy the show so much that they keep coming back for more."

"Yeah, I guess."

"Well, Erin, my friend, the time has come to give the viewers that extra little twist that they love. No more lounging around by the pool, making love all day..."

My face flames.

"Don't," Wade says. "You don't have to do this."

"He's right," Graham says.

"Sorry, boys, it's my job on the line here and it's my call to make. If I can't please the people, I'm out, and let's just say better your asses than mine."

"What is it?" I demand. "Leaving us here alone to die without food and water isn't enough? What else could they possibly want from us?"

Andrew laughs. He actually *laughs*. "You three are all that's left. And now, two of you need to die."

"What?" My head is spinning. I don't think I heard him correctly. The others seem to be somewhat less stunned than me. "You knew this would happen," I say to them. I want to vomit. Nausea overcomes me, and I lean over to dry heave.

"We never knew it would go this far," Graham says. "I swear it, Erin. This isn't what we signed up for."

"You knew something. Why else fight me so hard not to get over here?"

"We didn't know the ship would leave us. After that, I knew something was wrong. The smoke—I knew not to trust it."

"You should have said something! Anything—"

"I tried! Erin, I'm so sorry." He runs his hands through his hair. "He said we wouldn't get paid if we talked about it. I knew not to trust him but I thought—I thought if we were going through all this, I better at least get fucking paid for it. I didn't want to risk it."

"Because your paycheck was more important than being honest."

Wade doesn't speak, doesn't confirm Graham's words, but the look on his face tells me he feels the same. He charges toward Andrew with murder in his eyes.

"Kill me, and you'll never get off the island!" Andrew yells just as Wade takes a swing.

"I might not anyway," Wade says. He gets one good hit in before backing off.

Andrew wipes blood away from his nose. "That's what I thought," he says. "I'm the only way any of you get out of here. If something happens to me, the investors will let you all die. There will be no survivors, not even the one."

The three of us look at each other. "No one else is going to die," I say. "None of us. We'll find another way."

"I wouldn't be so sure about that," Andrew says, smiling back at Wade.

"He's right, Erin," Wade says. He turns toward Graham and attacks.

CHAPTER FORTY-THREE

Y OU THREE ARE ALL *that's left.* Andrew was telling me something—Wade was lying about the others. Everything was not fine. There *are* no others anymore.

I watch in horror as Wade attacks Graham. I wonder if this is how it happened with Lauren, Marcella, and Caleb. He attacked them, killed them all? No, it couldn't have been so simple. I don't know why this is happening to us, why Graham or Wade would agree to anything like this, but I don't believe either are cold-blooded killers.

Andrew slinks off behind the tree line to watch us from who knows where. I could run. I could get away. I could follow Andrew to see where he's going. Or I could stop this madness.

I can't just leave them. I can't leave Graham to fight for himself while I run. It would make me almost as bad as Andrew.

"Wade, please!" I cry. "Don't do this again. Please stop." He ignores me. They both do, *just like before.*

This time, there's not just going to be broken bones. Something much worse is going to happen. This time, there's something different. Their fighting is more animalistic, rawer.

Graham is injured, was barely able to walk on his own before, but the adrenaline has given him enough strength to keep up with Wade's onslaught. For now.

Wade throws punch after punch, aiming for Graham's weakest spots. When he gets close enough, he tries to get Graham in a choke hold, but Graham is a master evader.

"We need to be smart about this. I know we can do it," I say. "Please stop!" I cry again. I may as well be shouting into the wind.

Fear starts to overwhelm me. Wade is really going through with this. I'm about to witness a murder in cold blood. *How can he just do this without even trying to find another way? I'll be next.*

"Get out of here, Erin, before you get hurt," Graham says.

"I'm not going anywhere without you."

"How touching," Wade sneers.

I look at him, floored by his tone. It's so unlike him I almost feel like I imagined it.

"Wade, this isn't you."

"And how the fuck would you know who I am?" he says. His eyes flick toward me for a split second, giving Graham the opportunity that he needs.

Graham kicks Wade in the kneecap with all the power he has left. Wade screams, not quite drowning out the sound of his leg breaking. He goes down hard, landing on his side.

I'm on pins and needles as I wait for Graham to make his next move. We've grown so close over the past weeks, I don't want anything to happen to him. I can't stand to watch him do something so stupid, so cruel though.

Maybe I never really knew him at all, just like Wade said. Graham could've told me about all of this. He could've warned me. How many times when we were together did he have a chance? Too many. And he didn't take one of them. How can I possibly know what he'll do now?

He hovers over Wade, thinking about his next move. Both men are bleeding and broken, neither who I thought they were. *Are they even writers?* Now I can't even be sure of that.

"Graham—"

He doesn't look at me, doesn't respond.

"Graham, don't do this. We can—"

He kicks Wade in the face before standing on top of his chest. In his hand, he's holding the flare gun.

Wade gasps for air and tries to get out from under him, but Graham pushes harder into his sternum until his bones start to crack. Wade is pinned in place, helpless.

"Graham! No!" I scream, all the blood draining from my face. I feel like nothing is working. My lungs don't want to bring in air, my legs don't want to move. All I can do is stand and watch.

Graham doesn't even glance my way.

Wade meets my gaze. "Run," he says.

Graham aims the gun and then pulls the trigger. The flare shoots straight into Wade's face, killing him instantly. His body catches fire and Graham takes a few steps back to watch him burn.

Before he thinks to turn toward me, I back away quietly and run.

CHAPTER FORTY-FOUR

I DON'T KNOW where to go. I don't know what to do other than to run. There's no one left, no one to trust, no way out.

As I scramble back through the forest, trying to put as much distance between Graham and myself as possible, I think about my life and what it's become. All my years of existence have led me to this moment. What could I have done differently? Probably a thousand different things. A million, even.

I almost laugh at myself for thinking of my ex-husband. Matt would've found a way out of this. That's what he does—he's a fixer. I wonder if maybe I threw our marriage away for the wrong reasons. Was it really that bad? Sure, I was lonely, but was it worth throwing away everything? Right now, I'd give anything to be back there instead of here.

Less than five minutes after running, Graham calls to me. "Erin, I'm sorry you had to see that."

He's not far.

I wind my way back the way we originally came, then cut over to backtrack in the opposite direction. I want to head farther down the beach to cover ground I haven't been yet, but if he's tracking me, I'm hoping to confuse him. I don't know what he's really capable of—never really did.

Would he really hurt me? After everything? Seeing what he did to Wade, how he didn't even flinch—I think he would want to get off this island, especially if he feels it's the only way.

"Erin, I'm not going to hurt you," Graham calls, seeming to read my mind.

I want to call back, to talk to him, ask him so many things. That could be what he wants too. If he's smart, he's going to try drawing me out. I can't let that happen until I at least have a way to defend myself.

I keep moving, faster than I'm comfortable with considering the terrain, but knowing he's injured and can't keep up. The stench from Wade's burning body makes me gag as I run past. My vision grows blurry with tears, and I force myself to go faster, farther, until my lungs are barely able to take in enough oxygen.

Finally, when I'm so tired I can barely stand, when I'm so thirsty I can barely swallow my own saliva, I stop. I allow myself time to rest, willing my thirst to go away. I have a single water bottle—half-empty, no food, no supplies. Graham and Wade had everything else.

I force my breathing to slow so I can listen. I can't hear him anymore. *Did it work?* There's no way for me to know for sure. He might be listening for my movement too.

The sound of the waves lapping against the shore is close. If I move onto the sand, I might be able to get my bearings, see if there's another dock. *Maybe even find Andrew or these investors.* Or not. They may be farther inland, but it makes sense they would have their own method of transportation. They're not going to trap themselves here with us.

With my plan in mind, I step out onto the sand, knowing

Graham will be able to track my footprints. I try to cover them as I go but doing so is time consuming. Even if he's not close now, he will be soon and anything I'm able to cover is better than nothing. *Hopefully it's good enough.*

There may be more lounge chairs over here, more tiki umbrellas—maybe something I can use to defend myself with. If I have to break the chairs apart and make a damned wooden stake, that's what I'll do.

I allow myself a couple of sips of water before moving on. When I reach the shore, what hope I had of making any kind of weapon is crushed. There are no more tiki huts or umbrellas or anything else. There's nothing but sand and water and palm leaves all the way into the horizon.

As I'm scanning the horizon, trying to pinpoint if there's another dock or not, something catches my eye. There's movement in the water. Something—something misshaped, floating.

Using my hand to block the sun from my eyes, I focus on the object out at sea. It's bobbing up and down with the waves, seeming to come closer but it's hard to tell. It must be driftwood or something.

I start to turn away to bring my focus back to the island, when I hear something so faint, I do a double take. It sounded like *hello.*

I look around me first, to make sure Graham hasn't found me yet. And when the coast looks clear, I yell at the figure in the water. "Hello?" I jump up and down, waving my arms as high as I can reach.

When the figure moves, I can see the outline of arms waving back at me. I cover my mouth, shocked to my core. *Someone is actually out there.*

I start screaming louder, moving around in big movements to try to make myself clear to the person out there. It's definitely not a boat that they're on—or if it is, it's a tiny one. I don't know who it is or how they got out there, but I'm glad to see another living person.

The only problem now is Graham. How long will it take for him to find me? And do I just wait here for this person to get here, or do I keep moving?

CHAPTER FORTY-FIVE

I DECIDE to use some time and clear as many of my footprints from immediate view as I can. If Graham sees some of them, it'll look like I disappeared into thin air, and it might give me enough time to spot him before he spots me. That is—if he shows up before whoever it is out there on the water.

I can't believe this is happening. I want to scream at him, cry, hit something, wail like a baby until I can get this emotion out of my chest. *How did I not see it?* How was I so blind? I trusted him more than anyone and he's—he's a killer. A liar.

Sitting at the base of a palm tree, I shove my misery to the back of my mind as I watch the person in the water grow closer and closer until I'm able to clearly make out that it's some kind of makeshift raft. I gasp when I see it, realizing what it is. *That's what was going on with the others.* Wade didn't kill them, or at least not all of them. Someone got away, and he didn't want me to know.

The person on the boat starts waving and yelling again and I can see now that it's Marcella. I start to yell back at her —she's almost to shore now—but I realize she's not talking to me. Graham is on the beach, waving back to her.

No, no, no! Shit! If I yell at her, he'll spot me, and I'm dead. If I don't warn her though, he's going to kill her. She has no idea what he's done, what he'll do to her.

She killed Tom. I pause, torn and confused. *What do I do?* I could've heard wrong—Lauren never said the exact words... but what if I'm right? Either way, I can't stoop to that level. I can't leave her for Graham without a fighting chance.

At least I'll have a chance to run for it. Marcella won't. "Don't come to shore!" I scream at the top of my lungs. "It's not safe!" I run out from under the tree, waving my arms at her again. From the corner of my vision, I see that Graham is walking toward me. I stay to repeat my words one more time, then I run.

"Erin, stop!" Graham calls after me.

"Erin!" Marcella's voice is clear now. She's close enough to swim the rest of the way in if she wants to. It seems she has no way to control the raft, or at least none that I can see. The waves are bringing her in whether she wants them to or not.

I stop running. Graham, who was almost on my heels, stops too. "Let me explain," he says, breathless.

"There's nothing to explain. I know the situation we're in. You didn't tell me. You killed Wade, and you're going to kill me in order to get out of here."

He grimaces at my cold tone, but I don't care. *How could I have ever trusted him?* "I'm not going to hurt you." He says, reaching for me.

"Why would I believe you? You don't have an alternative. If you want to get out of here and get paid—" I shrug. "I know what you have to do."

"Dammit, I wish you would listen!" he screams. "Just fucking stop and listen!" He lurches forward, grabbing for my arm. I try to evade his reach, but I'm just slow enough that he scratches me. His fingernails are long enough and sharp enough to draw blood.

He either doesn't notice that he hurt me or doesn't care because he reaches for me again and this time he grabs hold of my wrist and squeezes. "Let me go!" I cry, trying to yank myself free.

Graham's grip tightens on me. He uses his other hand to squeeze into my shoulder, making me feel like a pinned beast. I swing at him, furious that he would hold me down like this, scared to death of what he's going to do.

I hear the sound of splashing in the water, but I'm too focused on Graham to look at Marcella. "You're hurting me!" I scream, almost into his ear, and he finally gets the picture. His grip loosens, not completely, but enough for me to pull my arm free.

"I'm not going to hurt you," he repeats.

"You already are."

He holds his hands up. "I just want you to listen."

Marcella reaches the shore, flops over on the sand with a small bag in her arms, out of breath. "God, that was a work-out," she says.

"We have to get out of here," I say to her.

She's staring at the sky and doesn't seem to be taking me seriously. "I know," she says.

I look at Graham and then back to her. "You know? What do you know?"

"Wade is going to kill us all."

"He's dead," Graham says.

She pops up at that, finally looks at us and sees the condition that we're both in. Graham lowers his hands to his sides, but Marcella is finally starting to understand there's something going on. "Oh." She stands and comes to me. "I think we better go."

I look at Graham again. "I'm going with Marcella. Don't follow us."

He shakes his head. "Don't do this, Erin. It's a mistake."

"Just like following that smoke? Why? Because you know I'll find out something you don't want me to find out?"

"No—"

"We're going." I take Marcella's arm and lead her on the beach. I'm slightly surer that he's not going to kill us—he could've easily done it already if he wanted. But maybe he's giving the viewers something to think about.

CHAPTER FORTY-SIX

MARCELLA and I find ourselves camping on the beach at night. We decide to stay out in the open so that if Graham decides to approach us at least he won't be able to sneak up. I dig my bare toes into the cool sand as I relay everything that's happened to Marcella—everything they told me about the cameras, the reason we're here, about how she was supposed to be dead, about what Graham did.

It's hard to keep from crying. I force myself to keep the tears at bay though. I refuse to break down in front of her.

"I'm so sorry, Erin," Marcella says. "I should've never let you leave with Graham. I should've done something. I was such a bitch and I'm the one who dragged you into this mess."

"It's fine. You didn't know." I shrug off her words, but inside I'm glad she's finally acknowledged her responsibility in this.

"Everything makes more sense now," she says. "I knew something was going on when Andrew showed up and—what he did to Lauren." She grimaces and clenches her eyes shut at the memory.

"He—killed her?"

"Yeah. Shot her without a warning." Wade and Caleb acted like nothing was wrong. "Build the raft—business as usual."

I shut my eyes too, trying not to picture what she went through. "They thought they were fooling you, I suppose."

Marcella surprises me with a shriek of laughter. "You should've heard the worry in Caleb's voice when he was screaming for me to come back with the raft. I almost fell off from laughing so hard."

I'm a little confused by why she would find that so funny. Warning chills run up my spine as I nod.

"Marcella—I'm not sure how to tell you this—" I'm wary of her, from both her attitude and the conversation I overheard. She's my best friend but there's no way to predict what she'll say or do. If she loses it right now, it's just the two of us.

She raises her eyebrows, waiting for me to continue.

I inch back a little. "I—overheard a conversation between Lauren and Caleb. Lauren suggested... that you killed Tom."

"She what?" Marcella flushes, looking horrified. "And you believed her?"

"No! Well—yes, maybe. I don't know."

Marcella comes toward me, bridging the gap I tried to create. She holds my shoulders while looking me in the eyes, the most sincere I've seen. "I did not kill Tom."

I bite my lips together, nodding. Every word could be a lie. I'm not sure but I know I'm stuck with her for now. She and Caleb were supposed to be both killed by Wade, according to Andrew. *That must mean*— "What happened to Caleb? Did Wade really kill him?"

"There was a struggle between them. Caleb tried to kill Wade, pulled a knife on him and everything. But he underestimated him, and Wade killed him first."

I frown, my confusion only growing worse. "You were able to see all that from the raft?"

Marcella is silent. She looks at me in a way I've never seen before. *In a way that I don't really like.*

"You know, you've always been like this. I can see why Matt wanted to divorce you."

My jaw drops. I stare at her, not knowing what to say. *Did I just imagine her saying that?*

"Oh, don't look at me that way," she says.

I stand up to move away from her. "I don't know what *way I've always been,* but you're out of line." I dig my fingernails into my palms, wanting to slap the look off her face.

Marcella stands with me and sinks her nails into my arm to keep me from moving. At the same time, she reaches for the small bag beside her, opens it, and pulls out a satellite phone.

I go numb, my body shaking as if in shock.

Marcella grips it with her free hand until her knuckles turn white, then holds it up to shake it in my face. "While you've been busy spreading your legs, I've been keeping in contact with Andrew, you dumb bitch. You think we're friends? All you are to me is a paycheck. And now you're asking too many fucking questions." She reaches back and punches me in the face with the hand still holding the phone.

It cracks against my face. Blood sprays from my nose down onto me and onto the sand. My eyes water from the pain. I shuffle backward, but she still has hold of me and won't let go. I use my other arm to swing at her, to scratch, to push her off any way that I'm able, but I'm nearly blinded by tears and blood.

"Get off me!" I scream.

Her nails dig in harder, so I reach for her hair, grabbing the biggest fistful I can. Marcella yells in outrage but hangs on. She reaches for her back pocket, and I pull down on her hair with all my might, putting every last bit of strength into it.

Marcella howls and finally releases my arm to reach for her hair. I let go of her and run. My arm has five bloody holes, my nose might be broken, and one of my eyes is starting to swell shut, but I run like my life depends on it.

"Erin!" Marcella screams. "Come back here, bitch!" She's after me, not far behind from the sound of her. *We used to run together, but it was never like this.* What happened to my friend? Or was she ever really that?

She's gaining on me. I look over my shoulder for a split second to see she's got something in her hand. It looks like a stick sharpened into a lethal point. If it's not that, it's got to be something close. She's out to kill me now too. She's in on it—knew everything already. Was only biding her time.

I turn back around. But it's too late. I step on something with my bare foot—something I didn't see because I was too busy looking behind me. I scream and drop, barely saving myself from landing on my already broken face.

I try to crawl, but it's pointless. Marcella is on me in seconds. She kicks my stomach and I fall again, heaving for air. She hovers over me with a disgusted look on her face. "What a waste of time," she says. "I was hoping to kill you in your sleep."

I try to move but she pins me in place. "Marcella, you don't have to do this!"

"Oh, but I do."

I hear a boom—the flare gun. The air behind Marcella lights up in a stream of red as the flare sails into her. She opens her mouth, but nothing comes out. Her shirt is on fire, but she doesn't notice. She falls to the sand—dead.

I back away from her, stunned. *I should be dead right now, not her.* She was seconds from doing it.

"Are you okay?" Graham says.

"You saved me."

"I told you I wasn't going to hurt you."

I look at him, see him. *He's not going to hurt me.* "How'd you know?"

"She just—" He shrugs. "Had this look. I saw her and Wade meeting and overheard them talking. I knew she knew."

So that's why they met in the forest. I grab his hand. "Thank you. I'm sorry I didn't listen."

"We need to find Andrew."

"We could just get out of here. Marcella's raft is out there somewhere—"

"No. It's gone. I don't think she ever meant to get far with it. And if we do somehow get out of here, they'll never let this go. There's only one way, and that's to find Andrew."

I bite my lip. I'm not sure if he's right about that being the only way for us, but I trust him now and I'm ashamed I didn't before. *We need to find Andrew.* "Okay," I say. "Let's do this."

Before we leave, we find the phone shattered on the sand. Graham tries to work it but it won't turn on, either from a dead battery or being busted on my face, there's no way to tell.

CHAPTER FORTY-SEVEN

WE KEEP WALKING down the beach the same direction we've been headed the entire time. From the view, it looks like we're now on the complete opposite side from where we started. The cliff that had been such a challenge for Graham and me to figure out looms in the distance.

I'm half-numb with the betrayal, the insane *game* that these people have been playing. If I get out of this alive, I'm not sure I'll be able to trust another stranger ever again. How can I after this?

Matt comes to my mind again. He wasn't always there for me, but at least I knew where his heart was. He was reliable when he actually was present. I couldn't imagine him putting his life in a stranger's hands the way I've done. I always thought he was uptight for being that way, stuck up even. But now I can see he was just smart.

There are no signs of life here and I wonder if they even put cameras on this side of the island. Dropping us on the other side, they may not have even expected us to get this far. It could be a reason they dropped us off on that side, and if that's the case, we can use it to our advantage.

Graham and I turn with the island, and when we're around the bend, we stop. There's a small wooden dock that stretches out into the sea and tethered to it is a boat.

Graham and I look at each other. "Pinch me," he says.

I do it, and then I pinch myself.

He whoops. "We're not dreaming."

"Is it him?" I say, unable to believe that what we've been hoping for is actually in front of our eyes. *Is it actually over?* Something tells me it won't be so easy to get what we want out of him.

"Has to be. Who else would it be?"

GRAHAM and I walk as softly as we can across the dock, trying to keep the element of surprise on our side. If there *are* cameras, we still haven't seen any. But we both know that doesn't mean much. For all we know, they could've put them on every square inch of this island.

There's no one on the deck of the boat that we can see. We step aboard and hold our breath for someone to come out and try to murder us. When no one comes, Graham motions toward a door.

It's a small boat for one that goes on the ocean, but still big enough to have a cabin underneath. Graham and I eye the door. There's no movement. No one is coming.

Graham nods, whispering, "You first or me?"

I reach for the door handle, bracing myself. Then I swing the door open. There are three steps to take me down into the cabin. It's dark, but I see a bed from where I stand. I look back to Graham for confirmation.

He nods to me again, giving me a thumbs-up. There's no way to defend myself if this is a trap. All I can do is hope for the best and count on Graham to have my back. This would be a hell of a time to betray me.

"Everything okay?" he whispers from behind.

"Yeah," I whisper back. Then I go down the steps.

There's a small living area with a couch and a TV, a desk, and a bathroom. And no one is here. The boat is empty. "Where the hell is he?"

Graham starts opening drawers and cupboards, looking for anything that might give us a clue. "Go see if the key is in the ignition," he says.

I run back up top and move to the helm. *Please let it be here!* I don't know anything about boats, but I'm assuming the key is in the same place the driver sits—just like in a car. There are buttons, switches, and a lever, but no key. *Nothing.*

"Can I help you with something?" a voice says.

I scream, nearly jumping out of my skin when he comes up behind me. I turn to see Caleb alive and well and grinning.

PART 7

CALEB

CHAPTER FORTY-EIGHT

Iᴛ's funny how much you never really know a person. You can spend weeks, months, even years with someone and never know every little thing. For instance, Wade and the others spent so much time with me, practically up my asshole every day for weeks, and none of them had a clue about my experience with swimming.

In high school, I was a swimmer. In college, I got into free diving. Holding my breath comes as second nature to me, and I'm one of the best.

I let my body relax, loosening every muscle from my face down to my toes. Wade loosens his grip on my neck, feeling the fight leave me. Bubbles leave my mouth. From beneath the waves, I watch him swim away, sure he's killed me.

I let myself sink lower, and urge my body to fight the natural instinct to surface for air. Seconds pass and still I wait. When my lungs feel as if they'll burst, I still wait, pushing them further than they've ever gone. I stay beneath the surface until I pass my own record and only when the darkness is creeping into the sides of my vision and I'm sure I'm on the verge of death, do I resurface.

Wade is a blip in the distance, headed toward the shore. *If he looks back, will he know I'm not a floating corpse?* I only allow enough time for my lungs to refuel before I dive back under.

Beneath the surface, I swim farther out. If he looks back out here from the beach, I want to be invisible. Good ole Wade got the better of me this time but if he believes I'm dead, it gives me the upper hand.

As exhausted as I am, how utterly *done*, I know I can't stop. Part of me doubts Wade will even bother looking back in my direction—he'll be too worried about moving on. But if I'm wrong and he does look and does see me, what then?

I'M FAR ENOUGH out that when I look at the beach, I only see vague outlines of our camp. I should be nearly invisible now. I bob in the water, really hoping I don't see a shark fin coming my way. I may have a few skills, but fighting a shark isn't one of them. Now the question is, *how long should I wait before heading back?*

After floating for what feels like hours, I turn in the opposite direction to look out at the open ocean. I squint. *Is that—I* gasp, almost choking on water. *Holy shit, there's something out there. It's coming closer. It's a—a boat!*

I raise my hands out of the water, forgetting all about being discreet. If there's a boat, that means we get to go home, and all the bullshit is over. "Hey, over here!" I yell, still waving.

Water splashes in my face and goes halfway down my windpipe. I don't think they'll be able to hear me over the engine and ocean, but it's still worth a shot. I try to rise out of the water as much as possible, halfway jumping out like a dolphin.

The boat continues straight for me, to the point that now I'm starting to wonder if I should maybe move out of the way. It draws nearer. It's so close now that I can see the outline of a single person on board. *It can't be....*

The boat comes to an abrupt stop feet from me, sending waves over my head. I cough and fight to keep myself above the surface until the water levels back out. I shield my eyes against the sun when a figure leans over the side.

"Need a ride?" he says. *Andrew.* I should've known.

"Are you here to help me or kill me?"

"That remains to be seen." He chuckles when I stay put. "Oh come on, I know you must want out of that water. You have to be exhausted after the exchange with Wade."

He saw that too I suppose, although I'm sure he doesn't have cameras on the ocean floor, so he would've only seen our little scuffle on the beach. "Alright. I'll come up." I move to the back of the boat where a ladder hangs into the water.

After I've pulled myself up, Andrew throws a towel at me. He watches me dry myself off and then casually says, "Thirsty?" he opens a mini-fridge and pulls out a bottle of water.

Tears spring to my eyes. He has to know what he's doing to me and enjoys every second of it. I reach for the bottle wordlessly. It's the best water I think I've had in my entire life.

"Now, time to go before Wade decides to turn around," Andrew says. He moves back to the helm and pushes the throttle until we're well on our way. It seems he's headed toward the other side of the island. There's a moment where my body protests. A jolt of adrenaline shoots through me, my brain screams, *No, not back there!* But I tell myself, *Do I really care that much? He's paying me, he's giving me food and water. Everything is fine now.*

Andrew has to have some other agenda, some other plan for me or this wouldn't be happening. Has the plan changed so much? I wonder if any of the others are dead.

"Did you see Marcella?" I ask.

"Yes."

"Did she see you?"

"She's around the other side."

That's not really an answer. I decide not to push it. This is his baby, not mine. If he's okay with Marcella floating away on her little raft and he's not chewing my head off for not stopping her, fine.

"We have some things to discuss," Andrew says.

"Yeah, I figured."

"I hope you don't mind camping out with me for a while."

"Not if it means there's food and water. And maybe a little more cash."

He grins. "Don't worry, my friend, you'll be well cared for."

CHAPTER FORTY-NINE

ANDREW DIRECTED us out to sea so that we could come up on the opposite side of the island without being seen and is now pulling up to a small dock. It appears to be almost identical to the one we originally came to when we first reached the island.

A picture of Lauren with her hair blowing in the wind and an arm around my waist comes to mind. She was so excited to get our little group over here, thought it would be the most *daring* thing. *Yeah, it was daring, all right.* That woman was fun, but god, the charade was exhausting. I'm glad it's over now. It's a relief having the only person who knows what really happened to Tom, gone. *Besides Andrew and the cameras...*

I was only trying to scare him—following the group when they thought they were leaving me alone on the beach, waiting for the others to leave him, her, and Marcella alone. Then when Marcella made herself busy—I took the opportunity. Lauren was losing her shit over it, couldn't live with the guilt, kept thinking I was going to kill her too or someone else. It's like a weight off my shoulders not having her drag me down with her anxiety anymore. I wish this whole thing was over already.

"Home sweet home," Andrew says, smiling as he ties us to the dock.

"Care to tell me why we're back here and not far, far away?" I say. I'm so sick of this island, the thought of being here any longer makes me physically sick to my stomach.

"We're here because we're told to be, and we're going to stay until told otherwise." All good humor has left him. He's down to business now and wants to make sure I know it.

"So, we're supposed to just hang out here? Or is there another plan I'm not aware of?"

"*You're* going to stay here, yes. I have other things to take care of."

I narrow my eyes at him. The first question that pops into my mind is, *why?* Andrew has been sneaky this entire job, continually adding on little clauses to what we originally agreed on. He goes from telling me, *easy money*, to telling me I don't have a choice one way or another. He adds on that, *by the way, you're not going home until they say you can*, whoever the hell *they* are. Now he wants me to *stay here*.

"From the look you're giving me, it seems you're not happy with the situation," Andrew says. "Frankly, Caleb, that comes as a surprise to me. Considering you were half starved and probably going to die of dehydration, I would think you would be thrilled right about now."

"I am. I'm just eager to get home, that's all."

Andrew nods like he understands and even cares. "I'll let you in on a secret. If there's no *group of writers* left, there's nothing for the viewers to watch. So, no point in being here at that point, right?"

"Are you saying—it's the last man standing?"

He shrugs. "I'm not saying anything. Just thinking out loud, that's all."

"I knew it. I knew you wanted us to kill each other."

"I'm not saying that," he says again, grinning this time.

"Why can't you just be straight with me?"

Andrew lets out a deep sigh. "I'm doing what I can. Now, before you can question me to death, I'm leaving. The house is yours; make yourself at home. Food and water are downstairs in the cabin or up here in the mini-fridge." He pulls the keys from the ignition and gets ready to leave.

"When will you be back?"

"I'm not sure."

"Do I have to stay on the boat?"

He shrugs, then steps off the boat and onto the dock. "Stay close."

"I don't understand the point of this!" I call when he's halfway down the dock.

He turns to call back, "Just a nice little surprise for whoever decides to show up." Then he's gone.

I COULD ALMOST LAUGH. I'm on a boat on a deserted island, but I can't leave. I sit back on one of the seats and look at my surroundings while I try to figure out what the hell I'm going to do. There's no way to know how long I'll be here waiting. At least I'm going to be more comfortable now. I won't have to starve to death, that's a plus.

What they want me to do—that's clear enough. Andrew doesn't have to say the words for me to get the picture. If I want out of here, I need to kill whoever's left. And he's expecting them to come to me. The question is: how fucking slow are they going to be about it?

Getting up, I decide to have a look at the cabin below. I may as well make myself comfortable, like Andrew suggested. There's nothing I can do now but wait until it's my time to shine.

EVERYTHING SEEMS UNTOUCHED—UNUSED. Everything from the lifejackets to the sheets on the bed looks like they were just bought, almost as if it's been staged. I wonder if someone actually went out and bought this boat for this sole purpose. With the amount of money these people are kicking around, I kind of wouldn't put it past them.

I spend my days aboard the ship, reading from the small selection of books, fishing, and swimming. To kill time, I take walks down the beach and sometimes go up into the forest before turning around and coming back.

There is no TV, no radio, no human interaction. There's paper and pen, that had to be left as a joke. I went into this *writer's retreat* knowing what would happen, but I still thought I'd get some writing done. I actually thought with having nothing else to do, I'd get a hell of a lot of it done. And how much did I get written? Nothing, that's how much. The one single day we spent writing, I was making an outline. What use is it to me now? Those pages are stuck back at the camp I'll probably never see again.

There's no way I can sit down and actually commit myself now. What do I do if someone shows up when I'm lost in my pages? Say, *Sorry, guys, hang on, just let me finish this paragraph.*

I toss the blank pages into the water, disgusted with myself for not being more productive. I promise myself, *When I get back home, I'm going to get back on track, write every damn day, and get this book done.* For now, I need to focus on surviving.

I leave the boat and head into the forest for a walk to clear my mind. I think about home and how long I've been gone. I think about my cat. I hope my neighbor is taking good care of her.

The sun dips, and my stomach starts to rumble. As I head back to the boat with lunch in mind, I begin to hear what sounds like a voice. My spine tingles. *Is someone finally here?*

I make it to the boat and see Erin searching for something. She's flipping every switch she sees, trying to get the boat started. *She hasn't even noticed me.*

"Can I help you with something?" I ask.

She screams and stares at me like she's seen a ghost.

CHAPTER FIFTY

"You're alive," Erin says.

I hold my hands up and twist from side to side. "All in one piece."

"How? Andrew said—"

"And you actually trusted him?"

Erin blushes. "Good point—I'm glad he was wrong. I'm glad to see you." She brushes tears from her cheeks and takes a step toward me, hesitating slightly. She hugs me, saying, "I knew Wade was a good person."

I almost laugh at the words. *Wade was a good person?* She doesn't know a thing about him—what he's done, what he was capable of doing. Just because she was willing to screw him, doesn't make him a good person.

I saw the way she looked at him before she left with Graham. God, she really got around our little group. I wouldn't be surprised if she had a thing going with Tom too. Hell, I shoulda got in on the action when I could.

Erin tries to let go of me, but I hold on to her. I lock my arms around her back and after a moment of still not letting go, she starts to struggle. "What are you—" She wiggles and pushes but I squeeze until her breath comes in short little bursts.

"You're so stupid, you know that, Erin? My god, woman."

"I take it you're in on it too," she says, gasping. *Finally catching on.*

I let the laugh out that I've been holding in. "You didn't think it was strange that I was here?" I squeeze harder, watching her face turn red from the pressure.

She shakes her head, can no longer speak.

"Hey, asshole!" someone yells.

A rope slips over my head and around my neck. I let go of Erin instantly, trying to get a hand between it and my skin but I'm too slow. Whoever has me yanks me back from Erin and twists until no trace of air can get through my windpipe.

I pull at the rope with everything that I have, I try to reach behind me, I try to grab *anything* for leverage, but there's nothing to grab on to. Nothing that will help. With each movement I make, I feel myself getting weaker.

Erin watches me in silence, rubbing at her own neck. Even struggling for my own life, I wonder what she's thinking. If she realizes that whoever my attacker is, they really did save her life. Another few seconds and she would not exist.

There's not going to be a savior for me. The edges of my vision are starting to darken. *So much for that free diving training.* All that discipline is good for nothing now. *Or... maybe not.*

My eyes flick from Erin to what's behind her. *The water.* As a last-ditch effort, with the last of my strength, I use my legs to push against the seat in front of me.

My attacker wasn't expecting the sudden reversal of direction. The rope loosens a fraction. I gasp. And we fall backward into the water.

The moment we hit the water, my throat is free. My

natural instinct is to rub at my raw skin, but I know I have to move. I have to get away, get my bearings so I can fight back. I don't have time.

Strong hands grip me and hold me down before I can surface. I didn't get enough oxygen in to outlast them, but I got enough in to fight. *If I'm going down, this fucker is going down with me.*

I drag myself closer to the boat's hull to use it as leverage. I'm able to turn and I finally see who my would-be killer is. Graham. *That son of a bitch.* Too bad I didn't have time to ask about Wade.

Our eyes meet. I smirk at the look on his face. *Like he's running out of air.* He doesn't try to surface though. He seems to know this is it, one way or another.

He takes one arm from me and reaches for something. I could almost laugh because honestly, what does he have that's going to do any good at this point? He's so weak now, I actually might outlive this idiot.

Graham finds whatever it was he was searching for. *The flare gun.* I let go of him, force his other hand free of me and swim. I'm too late. He pulls the trigger and blows a hole into my abdomen.

PART 8

ERIN

CHAPTER FIFTY-ONE

EVERY SECOND they're under the surface, I feel like I'm holding my breath right alongside them. The water is so clear that I can almost make everything out. Graham loses his grip on the rope when they fall but he seems to gain control back.

Come on, Graham. You got this.

My fingers grip the edge of the boat until my knuckles are white. I watch as they struggle with each other and fight to win the upper hand. *How long can they stay underwater?*

They move almost directly below me, and I lean over the side to get a better view. They've stilled now. *What's going on, Graham?*

I'm starting to sweat, not from the heat but from the possibility that Graham might not make it back up to me. What am I going to do if Caleb is the one rising from the water? He nearly killed me, and I'm not sure how I'm supposed to fight him off a second time.

A loud crack comes and the boat shakes. Blood is spreading in the water, clouding my view. "Graham!" I call. I wait, but there's no further movement. I think about jumping in for him, but what if it's his blood? What if Caleb is there waiting?

I pull myself onto the edge and brace to jump in. "I wouldn't do that If I were you," a voice says. I'm startled by the sudden appearance, but a hand grabs me before I fall in.

Andrew.

As soon as I'm settled back into the boat, I back away from him. "Where were you?" I say. "Caleb was here. He tried to kill me, and he's down there with Graham now."

"I know."

"You know? We have to help him. Please, we have to do something."

He offers me a tablet. "Look."

I take it with shaking hands and almost drop it when I see Graham on the screen. He's floating beneath the water, eyes wide open. Dead.

"I know," he says again.

My lip quivers. I try to control myself, but I'm not sure what to do. Graham has been my rock for the past weeks, and now—he's just gone.

"It's over," Andrew says, filling the silence. "You're the last one standing. Congratulations, Erin. Now, it's time to get the hell out of here."

"Just like that?"

He raises his hands in the air. "Just like that."

"We need to get Graham out of the water. I can't leave him like that."

Andrew presses his lips together and tilts his head. "I don't think you quite understand how this works. Let me explain." He strokes his chin. "When I say, 'It's over,' it means we leave now with nothing but the clothes on our backs.... that means no dead bodies."

"But—"

"Look at the amount of blood in the water. Sharks can smell that for miles out. They're probably already down there or not far off. There's really nothing I can do here, Erin." He checks his watch. "Now we really need to get going."

"Are we late for an appointment I don't know about?"

Andrew doesn't pay attention to the venom in my voice. "You have a ticket on a cruise home and if you don't make it, it's going to be a headache trying to rebook. Now, sit down and buckle up if you would." He pulls a key from his pocket and moves to the helm. Within moments, we're leaving the island I wasn't sure I would ever leave.

Everything feels hazy, like I'm in a dream. I could still be lying on the sand, dehydrated, dying from hunger or thirst or exhaustion. *What am I doing?* I look at Andrew, whistling to himself, driving us away from the island. It feels like déjà vu.

Why am I not stopping him? Am I really going to leave Graham like this? I look behind us to watch the dock growing smaller and smaller. *Is that a shark fin?* It's hard to tell now. I hate myself for not saying something else, for not doing something else. He saved me. He died protecting me.

I slump in the seat and close my eyes. "What now?"

"Now you keep what happened to yourself for the rest of your life. You know how these things go, or I'm sure you can imagine. If you tell, you die. And don't underestimate these people. They will find you."

"What about my family? My friends? They'll wonder where I've been."

"Tell them you went off-grid. Tell them whatever you want, whatever you need to, but *don't* tell them the truth. The investors are private people. I don't even know who they are or how many of them exist. Am I making myself clear here?"

"Yeah. I get it."

"Good. Because if you decide to tell a friend, you've just

murdered that said friend. Now, look on the bright side. You're alive, you're going home, *and*, the best part." He grins. "There's going to be a nice payday in your bank account—a nice little incentive, so to speak."

They're paying me to keep my mouth shut.

Andrew reads my mind. "You don't really have a choice, either way. So take the money and live your life. Otherwise..." He shrugs. "Like I said. It's over."

There's nothing else for me to say, so I stay silent. I flatten my lips into a fine line and bend to put my head between my knees. *One way or another, this is over.*

CHAPTER FIFTY-TWO

"YOU MAY AS WELL GO DOWNSTAIRS and take a nap or get something to eat. We have a few hours before we get there," Andrew says.

I stand to do as he says, not bothering to comment. If we have a long ride ahead of us, he's right—I may as well make myself more comfortable. At the mention of food, my stomach gives a loud growl. Anything other than bananas or mangos is going to be like a slice of heaven.

IN THE CABIN, something seems off. I can't quite put my finger on it, but I can sense it.

I find a fridge full of food and hesitate only a moment before digging in. If my fate is to die from eating poisoned food, so be it. Nothing is going to stand in the way of my stomach and some meat.

A moan escapes through my lips as I take a few bites of food and force myself to stop. I'm tempted to ignore logic and keep eating until I can fit no more in, but I know what will happen if I go too fast. I could wind up dying. *Wouldn't that be just the way to go?*

I step away from the food and over to the bed, and that's when I know what's wrong. The floor is squishing when I walk. There's water seeping in.

The food I just ate threatens to rise. I feel hot and clammy, close to losing myself to hysteria. *Andrew will know what to do.* Running back up top, I find him talking on a phone.

"Yes, sir, as instructed," he says.

"Andrew?" I say loud, hoping whoever's on the other end of the line will hear my voice. "You have a phone?"

His eyes flash a warning. He doesn't speak for a moment, focuses on what's being said through the phone's speaker. I strain, trying to hear too, desperate to tell him about the leak, but terrified of what the person is saying. He could ask them for help, but something tells me they may not want to send it. If a sinking boat in the middle of the ocean made for good viewing, they may just sit back and watch us drown.

"I understand," he finally says. "Thank you, sir." Andrew ends the call and then looks at me.

"We have a problem," I say before he can speak.

"Oh? What's that?"

"We're taking on water. A lot of it."

"I know. The boat is going to sink within a couple of hours."

"You—how do you know? Why are we going out to the open ocean if you know we're sinking?" My voice is steadily rising, along with my heart rate. *I actually survived this insane situation just to have this happen? What did I do in life to deserve this?*

Andrew sighs and actually rolls his eyes at me. "You know, Erin, I'm getting tired of repeating myself." He points to the tablet lying on one of the seats. "Remember, cameras everywhere?"

"Do the cameras tell you we're leaking?" I can't keep the dryness from my tone.

"Actually, smart-ass, yes, they do. They show when your lover boy decides to shoot a flare directly at the hull of the boat. There are also sensors that tell me when we're taking on water and the estimated time of sinkage. Don't think there's a single thing that doesn't escape me, Erin. I'm paid well to make sure I know everything."

"So what do we do? You knew about it already, fine. Please tell me you have a plan."

"There's a helicopter coming our way. We'll board it and that will be that."

"A—"

"That's right. So, we sit tight for now, and when the time comes, don't try to throw me under the bus again."

My face burns. "I wasn't—"

"You were." He turns to make himself busy.

TWO HOURS LATER, we've stopped moving. We've taken on so much water, we're barely staying afloat. I analyze Andrew's features, looking for an ounce of worry to appear. There's a flicker of something, but it's not worry. I almost think it could be *relief.*

"How much longer, do you suppose?"

He gives me a rueful smile. "They'll show when they show."

"You mean, *if* they show."

He only nods. It's the one honest response he's given me since I've met him, and it scares me to death. There's no way out of this if they decide not to show—no life raft, no other way to survive. The only thing we have is a life vest for each of us, to prolong the inevitable.

"Maybe this is some kind of joke," I say. "They want to make us sweat."

Andrew won't meet my eyes. He doesn't want to discuss this, I can tell. For all he or I know, there are more cameras aboard, microphones too. *Maybe they're testing him to see if he'll break.*

"We're not very far from one of the main islands," he says, changing the focus. "If we have to, we can swim. It's only another hour or two by boat."

"Why are there no other boats in the water? No planes overhead if we're so close?"

He places a hand against one of the seats, trying to shake it. "I don't know if we'll be able to pry the seats up. We might have a better shot with the cabin door."

"Why aren't you answering me? Are you really considering this? You really think they won't show?"

He breaks into laughter, so sincere that I almost crack a smile. "If they didn't want us to survive, we wouldn't. If they didn't send that helicopter, what they're really doing is sending a message. And no—it wouldn't be worth the effort to even try."

Chills run up my spine. The look on his face—something on the verge of insanity—makes it worse. "These people aren't gods."

Andrew opens his mouth to speak but stops. His smile widens, and he points to the sky. "Hear that?"

I listen. *There's a helicopter in the distance.*

CHAPTER FIFTY-THREE

I STAND on the top deck of a cruise ship on my way home. It feels so surreal being here. I thought I was going to a writer's retreat with a friend, not being lured into an insane life-and-death game to please some psychotic people with god complexes. How did I make it out? How am I the one who survived out of the seven of us?

The wind blows my hair back and I tilt my face up toward the clouds as we set off for Florida. I can't wait to be back home in Washington, away from the sun, away from the heat. I'm going to hide myself deep inside the forest, away in the pine trees. I'm not sure if I'll ever step foot on a boat again.

Wait until Matt hears about this. He'll build me a cabin just so I can get away—

The thought lodges itself in my mind. Andrew's warning rings in my ears. I can't tell Matt. I can't tell anyone. They've given me everything I need for a backstory, and if I don't make everyone believe it, if they even suspect something's wrong, my life and theirs will be in danger.

The other thing I realize is that my ex-husband is the first person I'm thinking of. He's the first person I want to tell, even if I can't. He's the first face I imagine seeing, the first person I imagine running to, hugging, crying into.

What was supposed to be a seven-day cruise has turned into an over three-week-long nightmare. It dawns on me that I've thought of Matt every day—every time something went wrong, every time something went right.

We were married for six years, it's only natural to think of him. But it's not just that. I think in a situation like this, you realize who you really love and who you don't. Who matters when your life is about to be over—who is the last person you think of, that's the person you belong with.

My eyes clench shut as I try to push the image of his face from my mind. *Why do I have to think about him?* It's over between us. It's been over. He made it clear that he didn't care, and he was perfectly fine with a divorce. Even if I wanted to go back to him, I have more pride than that.

"Passengers, may I have your attention, please?" An announcement comes on through the loudspeakers. "All cabin rooms are now ready. Thank you."

I pass so many cheerful people on my way to my suite—smiling faces, hands holding colorful drinks with little umbrellas, all people who are completely clueless. *Or are they?* How many of these passengers are in on the game? How many of them are watching me just as closely as I watch them? I wonder if it will be like this forever—me always looking over my shoulder. *Yes, it probably will.*

In my room, I find my phone and bag that were lost on the island. My phone is plugged into the charger and there's a little sticky note on top of my bag that says, "Found these. Try not to lose them again."

I'm glad I won't have to deal with Andrew's sense of humor anymore.

Part of me wants to throw myself on the bed and sleep

until this nightmare is truly over. Only a few more days until we get there. I can stay here, drink myself into oblivion, order room service until I gain back the weight I've lost, stay hidden away until we make it.

And then what, Erin?

There's no Marcella to catch a return flight with. There's no writing group to say my goodbyes to, to shake hands with, hug, thank for the great time and awesome memories. There's no one to go home to. Will Matt even notice? *Why should he?*

Another part of me thinks about the writing that I never got done—not just during this trip, but during my entire life. I have a few days still; I could get a hell of a start—the few pages I wrote are waiting for me to pick them back up. A sliver of hope runs through me. *I can still do this.*

Images of the others flash in my mind. *Lauren, Tom, Marcella, Wade, Caleb—Graham.* Were any of them even writers? I think so. Or if not practicing, they were in their hearts. Even Caleb. I hold my hands over my heart and whisper, "I'm so sorry, Graham." I hope he can hear me wherever he is.

I'm going to write. I'm going to do it for myself but also for Graham. He pulled me through, and he believed in me. He was a total stranger, but he still believed, and he convinced me that I could do it too. He was a friend willing to die for me, and I can never forget that. *This one's for you, Graham.*

But there's something I have to do first. With shaking hands, I turn on my phone. The screen goes white and then message after message after message appears. Ten notifications, twenty, fifty, appear on the screen. My heart stops in my chest. *They're all missed calls and texts from Matt.*

I'm sorry.

Can we just talk?

I'm such an ass. I should've been willing to talk. Please, Erin, it's not too late for us.

Please don't ignore me.

I know I deserve it, but I also know you still love me. I still love you, too.

I feel faint. I was wrong. I was wrong about so much.

I look at the most recent message. **If you don't call me, I'm going to file a missing person report.**

I steel myself, rehearse what I'm going to say over and over in my mind, then I press the call button.

PART 9

MATT

CHAPTER FIFTY-FOUR

At forty-one thousand feet in the air, my phone rings. I look at the caller ID—it's Erin. A hopeful smile spreads across my face. I've been waiting for this moment. I knew she would call, but I still don't know how the conversation will go.

I clear my throat before answering. "Erin! Thank God. I was getting worried."

"I'm sorry, I wasn't trying to ignore you. I—" A pause and then she continues. "I decided to go off-grid, stay a little longer, do some thinking, clear my head, you know?"

I release a sigh. "I wish you would've warned me. I was worried something happened."

"Honestly, Matt, I'm surprised you even noticed I was gone."

I feel my face heat, and I'm glad there's no one around to see my embarrassment. "What do you mean? Didn't you get my texts?"

Erin goes silent for a minute before saying softly, "I did. And—that's what I've been thinking about. Us."

I wait for her to continue.

"You—don't really mean it, do you?" She sounds on the verge of tears—good ones, I hope.

"I meant every word. I love you, Erin. I never stopped."

"You never cared. Never said you cared, never listened. You were never there. Why now? It's a little late, isn't it? Why are you doing this to me now?"

"It took losing the only woman I've ever really loved to make me see what an idiot I've been. Erin, please, let's just talk. Give me a chance to try and win you back. When will you be home?"

The phone is muffled as she tries to hide her crying from me. She makes some noises on the other end of the line, sniffles, and tries to control her breathing. I wait for her to continue, trying to pretend I don't notice the emotion in her voice.

"Okay," she says. "Let's talk. I'll be home in a few days."

I pump a fist in the air, gritting my teeth. *Yes!* "I'll be waiting for you to call the minute you get back."

"Matt?"

"Yeah?"

"Do you—want to pick me up when we get to port?"

I grin, knowing I've succeeded. "I'd love nothing more than that. I'll make the arrangements."

"Thanks, Matt."

"Hey, are you okay? You sound... a little off."

A pause and then, "Yeah. Just glad to be going home."

"Me too, more than you'll ever know. I've missed you."

A FEW DAYS LATER, I'm waiting to pick Erin up at the port in Miami. When she sees me, her face lights up like a firework—brighter than even years ago when we first met. I beam when she hugs me, thrilled to have her in my arms again.

"Did you get much writing done?" I ask, hesitating. *I've come this far; I can't mess it up now.*

She stands on tiptoes and kisses me. When she pulls back, she says, "Yes."

"I'm going to be more supportive. I've been too consumed with work, too unfocused on what really matters. From now on, I want to read every word that comes out of that beautiful mind."

Erin's cheeks flood with color, but she nods. She hugs me again. This time her hands roam up my back. "I've missed seeing you in your suit," she says, breathing me in. "Always so formal, no matter where we are."

I grin, nodding to the driver, waiting to open the limousine door. He ushers us into the back seat. "Thanks, Russ," I say as he closes our door, and soon we're off to the airport, where the plane is waiting.

My phone buzzes in my pocket. I wait, watching Erin for a moment. She's silent, contemplative, looking out the window. *What I would give to know what she's thinking.*

I take the moment to check my messages.

Cleanup taken care of.

That was fast, faster than expected.

Good work, Andrew. Expect a bonus in your account.

I tuck my phone back into my pocket and notice Erin watching me. She gives me a small smile when our eyes meet. "No rest for the wicked."

"It's going to be different. I swear it. I won't lose you again."

"Let's take things slow, okay?" She takes my hand in hers. "This trip made me realize how much I miss you, but I need time still."

I almost quip, *Maybe we should send you on a trip like this more often,* but I don't think she'd appreciate the comment. Besides, Marcella isn't around anymore to persuade her. *That was a solid investment—and good choice on giving her that phone.* Instead, I say, "Of course." I'm just thankful to have another chance, after all. I kiss her forehead and wrap my fingers tighter around hers, leaning back into the seat as we drive.

Erin leans her head onto my shoulder, and I close my eyes, enjoying every minute. I do a mental calculation of the cost to get to this moment. More than a small fortune. There's already been a payout of course—there always is, and it's usually immediate.

It's an investment, remember? I remind myself. And it's true. Even if I never saw a single dollar of it back, it would be worth it because I've won the real treasure. Erin.

I knew she would miss me. I knew when it came down to it, her life in jeopardy, on the verge of death, she would think of me. She would want me, value *us* again, remember how much we meant, how good we are together.

It was never even a gamble. I made sure she would be fine, and I made sure things would turn out the way they did. *Money can't buy happiness? Says who?*

When I open my eyes again, I struggle to keep a grin from spreading. I can't show my complete happiness yet. Erin is too smart, she'll catch on. This is the hard part—not seeing her on those monitors, not watching her make love to another man, not waiting for her to come home to me.

She needs to believe. And looking down at the top of her head, resting against me, I know that everything is going to work out just fine.

THANK YOU FOR READING!

Enjoyed Lost?

For a deleted scene from **Lost** sent to your email, sign up for the K. Lucas newsletter at
https://BookHip.com/PFSVRRX

Please consider leaving a review.

Reviews help authors more than you might think. Even just a few words make a difference and are greatly appreciated. The best place to review is whichever retailer you purchased from, but you can also consider Goodreads or BookBub.

ACKNOWLEDGMENTS

First and foremost, I'd like to thank my husband and son. Thank you guys for being my biggest fans, always offering encouragement after long hours of writing, and always being eager to listen to my next crazy idea. I love you both to infinity and beyond.

Thank you to my editing team at My Brother's Editor, for making my book shine and for being so awesome to work with.

Thank you to Angie, for helping me create the perfect blurb.

To my cover designer Dez, at Pretty in Ink Creations, thank you for giving me amazing covers every time. I look forward to each new creation that you make for me.

To my readers, you and your continued support mean the world to me! You are the reason I can continue doing what I love to do every day. You are the voice that echoes a little louder than my own, telling me *this is great!* Thank you for sticking with me, for encouraging me, fanning the flames, and for picking up each new book that releases.

Thank you dear reader, for showing me your support by reading this book. Whether you are new to my work or are one who keeps coming back for more, I truly hope you enjoyed the read.

ALSO BY K. LUCAS

The Wrong Stranger

The Neighbors

Rainier

I Am Not OK

Our Little Secret

You Kill Me

ABOUT THE AUTHOR

K. Lucas is a bestselling author who lives for the unexpected twist. Originally from California, she now lives in the Pacific Northwest with her husband, son, dogs, cats, and chickens. After earning a bachelor's degree in information technology, she became a homeschool mom and then a full-time author. She loves all things thrilling & chilling, and her favorite pastimes include reading, watching scary movies, and exploring nature.

www.klucasauthor.com

CONNECT WITH K. LUCAS

Connect With The Author!
See K. Lucas's website for more info, signed copies, and to sign up for newsletter updates!

Website:
www.klucasauthor.com

Newsletter:
www.klucasauthor.com/newslettersignup

To support future projects, get EXCLUSIVE behind the scenes content, sneak peeks, and more, find K. Lucas on Patreon.

patreon.com/klucas

amazon.com/author/klucas

goodreads.com/klucas

bookbub.com/authors/k-lucas

instagram.com/author_klucas

facebook.com/author.klucas

tiktok.com/@klucasauthor

pinterest.com/klucasauthor

twitter.com/AuthorKLucas